AF177000

Fools' Outing

Bernd is traveling with his wife through the Black Forest in Germany. Ellen's psychiatrist had suggested that this trip would help both of them psychologically. He was wrong. Her erratic behavior on this outing makes Bernd realize that he will have to leave her, if he is to save himself and their two young children from the emotional terror she has been inflicting upon them. For too long he has played the role of supporting husband, careful not to tear the mask off Ellen's face, he tells her psychiatrist, whereas she has no problem exposing him for his presumed inability to understand her.

Author

Udo Staber obtained his Ph.D. in organization science from Cornell University in the United States. He has held professorships at universities in the United States, Canada, Germany, and New Zealand. He has published numerous books and articles and has received a number of research and teaching awards. He currently lives with his wife in Stuttgart and Berlin.

More on the author: www.udostaber.com

UDO STABER

Fools' Outing

A Novella

Cover, Illustration: Udo Staber

Verlag: tredition GmbH, Halenreie 40-44 / 22359 Hamburg

ISBN

Paperback	978-3-7497-5897-5
Hardcover	978-3-7497-5898-2
e-Book	978-3-7497-5899-9

Our characters are the result of our conduct.

- Aristoteles

The Scream

You didn't think this trip would be hell for me, did you? But could it have been anything other than hell? Think about this, if you are up to it. Did you really believe that going on this trip would open up new possibilities for her, that she would discover a new side of herself, something different from her anxiety-ridden existence, that up-and-down roller coaster of emotions? Consider her rage and those feelings of betrayal she carries around with her. There is a history to this, you know, and this history doesn't disappear just because we are now in a different place or because conditions have changed. The past sets the premises for everything that happens today. In our case the premises are such that this trip would *have* to be a disaster. It was doomed from the beginning, it was doomed even before it started. Right here in your office it was doomed. Couldn't you see that, the frustration, the panic, that foaming drama of self-pity?

Most everyone faces despair at some point in his life. Just look at those desolate cases you are dealing with. But if I may say this, in all humility, you have no idea what despair means if you never had to spend a whole three days with Ellen and there is no escape. I'm not talking about spending a holiday weekend with her family or going to a faculty and spouse retreat with her. I am talking about something that you so bravely announced would be a vacation. She should look forward to a "vacation from her problems," you said. Well, this so-called vacation from *her* problems turned into a hell hole of problems for *me,* and this from the minute we stepped off the plane. What I went through every day, if you care to know, wasn't just some nightmare from which you wake up and that's the end of it. It wasn't an illusion either. It was real, and it was irrefutable proof to me that I have been living with a lunatic all these years.

Driving on the Autobahn is a grueling experience when Ellen is sitting next to you and you have an argument with her that makes absolutely no sense. When she insists that you give her your undivided attention because she has something very important to say, you just want to scream, but you don't because you think of yourself as an expert at self-control. What do you do when she starts one of her ridiculous arguments and you can't run away? Turn on the radio to distract her? Focus on the road, but otherwise drift into unconsciousness? Try to remember what you said about using a different mental filter to block out what she is saying?

Well, Doctor, I have run out of mental filters, I have done all your assignments, I have read every book and article you recommended, and I have followed every piece of advice you gave me. You told me it helps not to use words like should, ought, and must, but where do you think Ellen will get the incentive from to stop complaining about everything under the sun if I touched her arm ever so gently and said in a soft voice: Ellen, dear, have you considered how much better you might feel if you turned on the radio and listened to Mozart for a while? You know what she'd say? She'd tell me to listen to *her*. Then she'd rattle off her complaints about some neighbor, or one of my colleagues, or me regarding something I had failed to do or hadn't done properly. And whatever she is saying that's so important that not even "Eine kleine Nachtmusik" can quiet her down, she'd throw at you in her usual diarrhea-like flood of accusations and denunciations.

When she's like that I have always shown humanity. I have shown what you would call "strength of character." I have carried on, hoping she'd get better someday. But do you want to know what carrying on has meant for me? Yes, I have looked out for her, I have chauffeured her from church to church, and from doctor to doctor looking for some diagnosis that explains everything. All this is living proof that I care, while I'm downplaying my own misery. But living in misery and dreaming of a life without her hanging over me is not what I want. Please don't tell me dreaming is a good thing, that it's the royal road to the unconscious. I don't want to be in the unconscious, I don't want to *imagine* a new life. I want to *have* a new life, a life on *my* terms for a change.

I know this sounds harsh, but when we drove from the airport to our hotel there was a moment when I imagined how I would feel if I would pull over, give her a good push out the door, and then take off, burn rubber, as they say. No, don't worry, I would never do anything like that. I'm a civilized person, I hate violence. Even as a kid I fought with words, not with sticks. With Ellen all I do is imagine things. I imagine throwing her out of the car and I pretend feeling great when I drive off. You could say I survive on imagination. I have done this for years. One day I imagine she'll vanish, another day I imagine she'll get better.

But will she ever get well, Doctor? She's like having a third child to look after. I have cancelled classes to be able to sit with her in your office, holding her hand, for Christ's sake. If you knew how often I stay up all night, afraid she'll have a panic attack any moment. There have been times, when I had to ... Why are you grinning? I am talking about being worried sick, and you are giving me this face as if I'm a fool. Oh, it's so clever of you to talk about strength of character, about supporting her and being patient with her, but you are not in my shoes to know what it's like having to protect two children against a mother who abuses them and interferes in everyone's life at home in ways that turns everything into a goddamn mess, not to mention how she interferes in my work at the university. Considering everything that has been going on, I have done pretty well, I would say, but do you think I like playing hero? You said I should take one step at a time. Well, that's what I've done, for six years, lots of small steps, sometimes it had to be big steps, and look where she is now - and where it has gotten *me.*

In the car, when I asked myself this question, I was not the man I wanted to be, and I definitely was not a hero. I had no idea how to get out of this insanely irrational verbal fight. Some people would put a plastic bag over her head, you know. That morning, after our arrival in Germany, she wasn't just angry, she was sheer *terror.* Thank you for sending a terrorist to go with me on this trip. When she is in your office and she bombards you with her grievances, you can terminate the session if it gets too much for you. But being in a car with her I am at her mercy. I can't withdraw into anything that you so elegantly call "maintaining your personal space." There is only the car, and she is in it, and I'm going eighty miles an hour, with cars passing us on the left and an endless line of trucks on the right. I'm not able to shut her up, and I can't just drop her off on the roadside, for the simple reason that there is a law in Germany that says that on the Autobahn you can't stop to get rid of unwanted baggage.

Now, do you want to know what the argument was about? It was absurd, it was as absurd as organizing a dating club for cloistered nuns. The disagreement that started it was over something I had done in the airplane after landing, when we prepared to get off the plane. I was about to carry both our handbags down the aisle, when she yelled at me for behaving like the typical man showing off his glorious strength. She can carry her own bag, she said. I didn't say much, *she* was the one talking, saying that I was insulting her, that I was taking away her dignity, and that I was offending her intelligence, as if you need intelligence to carry a ten-pound bag when you have testosterone doing the work for you. She talked loud enough for everyone around us to hear her, as if she thought these people wanted nothing more than witness a woman being abused by her husband who wants to feel "manly" by snatching her handbag.

I think it was only ten miles outside the airport when she exploded like a volcano with a million years of pressure buildup behind it. I was doing it again, she said, taking control over *everything*. By "everything" she meant my driving the car, that is, holding the wheel, keeping one foot on the gas pedal, and looking into the rear-view mirror every few seconds. She felt deprived of all that, the poor thing. Forgive me, Doctor, I wasn't aware of what I had done. I should have asked her if *she* wanted to drive, she said. And I should have told the woman at the car rental agency, when she asked if I wanted two drivers to be registered, that she had an international driver's license. When I retorted that she should have spoken up – sorry, I said *should* –, she said she had been too tired after having had to yell at me in the airplane when I took her bag.

So that is how the great fight between your hypersensitive patient and her phallic perpetrator began, and it didn't let up until we reached Baden-Baden, the place where we spent our first night. In case you don't know, Baden-Baden is a city where people from all over the world normally go for rest and relaxation. They take in the fresh air from all those forests surrounding that place, they stroll through the expansive city park to admire magnificent floral exhibits, and they marvel at dozens of big buildings with those impressive Belle Époque facades. Many people visit the world-renowned healing spa to indulge themselves in a whole-body massage, and afterwards they jump naked into a Roman fresco decorated pool of warm water. That's what normal people do in Baden-Baden, but we are not normal. Ridiculous is a better word for what we are when she pulls me into an argument that makes absolutely no sense, and I end up screaming because I have run out of words.

What triggered her outburst in the car was what she saw in a car passing us. A man driving, ostensibly concentrated on the traffic around him, a woman sitting next to him half-dozing, and two children in the back seat playing games. Most people would see this as a happy family on an outing, but Ellen sees something else. "This man is driving so he can feel like a man," she says.

"What?!" Of course I know what's coming now.

"Oh, you know exactly what I mean." But just to make sure there is no misunderstanding she now gives me a quick rundown on what she learned in college about the typical family constellation as it has been since the rise of domesticity. You can be in the middle of postmodern society, but the family retains the old hierarchy, she says. "It's a fact" - you know how much she likes to speak in absolutes - "that *men* do the driving. You see women driving only when they are alone in the car, or with children, or with their elderly parents, but *never* when a man is with them."

"Sorry, but that's not quite true," I say, knowing that my objection will be the start of a major quarrel. I try to distract her by pretending that I'm in a good mood. It's August, this is the month when people go on vacation, and the weather is great, that's the message I want to send. "But who cares? I'm just glad we have such good weather today and it's not raining."

"I want to discuss something important, and you want to talk about the weather? How insensitive."

"Why? I just wanted to say that it's much easier driving in this heavy traffic when it's sunny and the road is dry." Sounds reasonable, doesn't it? "Why don't you sit back and rest. You could close your eyes and think about the nice days ahead of us."

Notice that I don't use words like should or must, but she is hissing at me nevertheless. "Don't patronize me, don't do that! I want you to take me seriously."

Doctor, look how she talks. Nothing but directives and commands. You could think I just stuck a finger up her nose. I talk like a good friend, but she sounds like someone who works for the Mafia and the KGB at the same time. We still have some way to go, another seventy miles or so, and the battle hasn't even taken off yet. I make her an offer: "Why don't you let me be your chauffeur today? I don't mind driving."

"I don't want to be chauffeured," she yells. "You are making fun of women."

"Sorry, how am I making fun of women? All I said is that you can relax, while I am driving. Close your eyes, if you want. That's not making fun of women. Or, if you don't want to rest, we could talk about something interesting, something more compelling than the question, who is driving, and why."

"There you go again. I want to have a normal conversation to discuss something that's important to me, your wife, but you know nothing better to do than make me feel like a nincompoop."

"I'm not *making* you feel anything, Ellen."

"Yes, you do. You don't know how you come across with what you are saying. You just don't get it."

"What don't I get?"

"It wouldn't do you any harm to develop more interest in women's issues."

"By talking about how chauffeuring you makes you feel like a nincompoop? Sorry, but aren't there more important things to think about when you discuss women's issues? Gender discrimination at the workplace, for example, or violence in the family." I mean it, Doctor. The former is a central topic in one of my courses, I could tell her about new findings. And regarding the latter I could easily come up with a few insights from sociological research on social deviance.

But there's no stopping Ellen once she gets going. "Women not being allowed to drive *is* a social issue," she says. "It's a symptom of abuse, something that is done to women everywhere. In all central areas of life women take the backseat, when they …"

"Backseat? You are sitting in front, aren't you?"

"Stop being sarcastic. You know exactly what I'm saying. When women are in the car, all they get to do is entertain the kids or study the roadmap."

To this I make a comment that I know I will pay for dearly. I mean it more as a joke, not as a provocation, but maybe I do want to provoke her. She needs a little provocation every now and then. It keeps her on her toes and it gives me the feeling of having at least some control over where this argument is going. "Study the roadmap? Come on, I know that women can read, but when it comes to roadmaps, they can't tell a highway from a railroad track."

Geronimo is on fire now. "Oh, this is so insulting. How dare you insult me like that! You think I'm stupid? *You* are the stupid one in this family. Only a moron would say something like this."

Now if you think that's the end of it, that she said enough for me to realize that I'm a moron, because it's true, I did say something moronic, and on purpose, you are wrong. She rants and raves for a good five minutes about the difference between knowledge and ignorance, reminding me that she had attended a women's college, a college for *intelligent* women, that is. Has she ever told you that she has a degree from a college for *intelligent* women? Well, now you know, so you can raise the level of intelligence a notch or two when you talk to her next time.

"Sorry," I say, trying not to sound too apologetic, "if you think the range of driving opportunities for women is an indication of their position in society, who can take you seriously?" I suggest we have a look at the next ten cars passing us, and without waiting for an answer I count how many of them have a woman in the driver seat. It's like the educational game I used to play as a four-year-old to learn simple math, except now it's serious, like getting everything right in one's last confession before execution. I count three cars with women drivers. "Three cars out of ten isn't much, but it's significantly greater than zero. So what does that say about women's position in society? Nothing!"

No trace of giving up. "I didn't say that women *never* drive," she barks back. "I only said that women never drive when there is a man sitting beside them."

"But in two of those three cars a man was in the passenger seat."

"Yes, and I bet that these men are going to take over the wheel as soon as they get a chance."

This conversation, if you can call it that, is grotesque, I know. I decide to treat her concern as something like a research question. This might be my only chance to get to the end of it in one piece. "You bet, but you don't know. You can't know what these men are thinking because you only see the outcome of a decision they made. They may have had well-thought-out reasons for not driving themselves, and maybe they made their decision after they discussed it with these women."

"I'm not going to waste my time arguing with you," she shouts.

"But *you* brought this up. *You* said that women not being allowed to drive a car is a symptom of a social malaise, something that women experience everywhere in this world. And you want me to take you seriously. Well, I do, so let's look at your suggestion that these two men are going to take over as soon as they get a chance. There is a lot we need to know before we can arrive at this conclusion. We need to study the actual process of making a decision, the articulation of preferences, the negotiation of competencies, the weighing of potential consequences, and much more. And most of the steps that make up a decision process are things that you cannot observe directly, so you end up speculating."

Ellen's logic in her answer is straightforward. "I don't need to observe anything," she says. "Everyone knows that men have big problems with women wanting to drive. It's the same with my father and with Bobby."

You should know that her mother has no particular desire to drive when her husband is with her. That's what she told me. And her brother is a special case in just about everything. Ellen knows that, but she draws the wrong inferences from it. "You cannot infer anything from just two cases," I say to her, "and you certainly cannot extrapolate from your family to the whole population." I briefly explain the small-sample problem. It's one of the dangers in sampling, when, for example, chance events are taken as typical and people arrive at distorted conclusions.

"I am not talking about some small sample. Just ask all those women who are married. If there is distortion, it's you who is distorting things. I am talking about a fact. It's a fact that men keep women from driving, which is what you are doing to me."

"Oh, I see, a fact, like the fact that your mother had a jolly good time playing pretty little bunny for your father and his priest friend."

"I am not answering this."

"Fine, so let's get back to the intricacies of a decision process. In those two cars, could it not be that there is something special about these men? They could be outliers, perhaps they are not *real* men. *Real* men have a problem with women. That's what you are saying, right? A *real* man would never let a woman drive when he is in the car."

Normally I'd feel ashamed for making a stupid remark like this, and for saying something I don't believe in. But these are not normal circumstances. For a moment she is quiet, then she says: "Maybe they are not their husbands, maybe they are a friend who treats them as a human being. Husbands would never do that, but friends would. Friends are always nice, that's why we call them friends."

Oh, these absolutes! Always, never. Do you see what I'm up against? All those facts I have to debunk. "But a minute ago you said that these men would be taking over the wheel."

"That was before I thought of the possibility that they are friends and not their husbands."

"And as soon as this friend becomes her husband he shows his true face and grabs the wheel. Is that it?"

She hesitates, then says without any trace of kindness: "That's what *you* would do, yes."

"Or maybe this man is ill and that's the reason why she is driving. She is nice to him, and he is grateful to her for that. A happy couple enjoying the warmth of the stronger one helping the weaker one."

"He is still a man. Wait till he feels well again, then he'll take control of the car because he ..."

"Because he is a *real* man, right? He doesn't want to end up in an accident, so he takes over as soon as he can. We should forgive him for this, he can't help it, he is mentally handicapped."

Although my eyes are fixed on the traffic ahead of us, I can sense that she is looking at me like a rattlesnake on attack, when she says: "Oh, you think you're so clever. To you this is all just a big joke."

"No, I'm serious. Do you really think a man who thinks this way lets his wife embarrass him in front of his male friends who most likely are just like him? Do you think he wants to be seen as some weakling who needs a woman to drive him around?"

Now you think this is ridiculous, two adult people, one with a Ph.D., the other one with a degree from a college for intelligent women, spending their vacation in a cockfight like six-year-olds arguing over who has the bigger marbles. And of course, it *is* ridiculous.

That's why you are treating her. How long has it been? Four years, five years since you started seeing her, and what has been accomplished in all those sessions? She's going bananas because she's not driving this car, and her husband, the great professor, widely published and winner of multiple awards, is helplessly seeking refuge in stupid sarcasm. If you had been with us in the car, what would you have said to me? Don't worry, don't take it personal, think positive, don't catastrophize? But look, I wasn't catastrophizing at all, this *was* a catastrophe.

The only chance of ending this silly dispute without losing my temper I see in dragging her into my professional métier, where I have a clear advantage over her. I could do a proper analysis of the situation, as I would do it with my students, helping them develop a few plausible hypotheses and using one or two theories to back them up. Proposing hypotheses, giving her something to think about, there is nothing wrong with that, is there? She should appreciate analytical thinking. She has a college degree, from a college for intelligent women no less. "Here is another hypothesis," I say. "The men in these two cars might be driving instructors."

She thinks about this for a few long seconds, then says: "Could be, driving instructors are always male."

I had meant this ironically, of course. On the other hand, in the social sciences it's okay to work with seemingly implausible hypotheses. In a field in which irrationality is the rule and certainty the exception far-fetched hypotheses might just turn out to be correct. As a social scientist you always want to be open-minded. It's no different in your profession, right? The conclusions we arrive at are always tentative, preliminary, and incomplete. That's what I teach my students. If you think you need a radically new explanation, for example when you are dealing with a few outliers, it's useful to formulate a really outlandish hypothesis. So that's what I did with Ellen, and I did it using a method I call "sarcastic reasoning."

"Right, most driving instructors are male. Women can teach fine arts, needlepoint, and gardening, but they cannot teach how to work with machines. And if we agree that men are machos, we can also agree that there is a conspiracy going on in the driver instruction business. It's men who keep women from becoming instructors. It all starts with men who think they are super clever when they act strategically and erect systematic barriers for women in the labor market, running through all social strata and occupational groups, but with fatal consequences for themselves who, given their macho stupidity and dedicated as they are to the principles of manlihood, thinking they are made of steel and can walk on water, have not considered the likely outcomes of their actions. The conspiracy ends with men having to drive themselves because they have turned women into zombies so bad that they can't even read a roadmap. They have to drive even when they are sick, half blind, or crippled from the waist down, and then they run the risk of hitting a tree. Maybe this is one reason why men have a shorter life expectancy than women."

With this I have clearly overdone it. I can tell from the way she expresses silence when she isn't sure if I'm being serious. I really would prefer having a sensible discussion with her, but that just isn't possible. Do *you* have rational discussions with people who talk about nothing else but needs and wants, and me, and me, and ME? All *you* do is listen, take notes, and draw your own conclusions, and what you are thinking you keep to yourself. That's the code in your profession. Well, I can't do that, I can't just take notes when she tells me the hundredth time that she has a degree from a college for *intelligent* women. And there is no law saying I must subscribe to the opinions of someone who tells me that she has an IQ of one hundred seventy-five.

I know that she isn't finished with me, and we still have another fifty miles to go. She is searching her brain for words that will put me in my place for the rest of the day. There is a good chance that those words will have something to do with the idea that has governed her thinking for I don't know how long, and that is that everything she has not been able to do in her life is something that men have prevented her from doing. It is men who have ruined her life chances, she says. Ask her, she might name some of those men for you. Her grandfather, for example, who molested her mother when she was a girl. And her father who kept a whole library of pornographic magazines under his bed; her grammar school teacher who reserved the lowest grades for the girls in the class; two husbands in the neighborhood who tried to seduce her mother when she was pregnant with Ellen's sister; the high school theater director who went after her when she was fifteen; her cousin who spent time in jail for having molested the five-year-old girl next door; and yes, there is the driving instructor who failed her in her practical test. And let's not forget the priest who shared with her father the special issues in his collection of Playboy magazines. Quite a distinguished family she comes from, I'd say.

If you care to know, I have been *very* sensitive to all this. I believed her stories and I shared her perception of these things, not just because I loved her, but because it's an ethical issue for me. I felt sorry for her, I looked after her, and I supported her. I concocted all kinds of excuses for her off-the-wall behavior when we were in company and people began turning away from her. I invented stories you wouldn't believe, out of concern for her reputation, not mine. Don't you think I went beyond the call of duty?

So why is she after *me* now? Because I'm too clever for her? Or because I'm too dumb for her, supporting someone who is so insecure about herself that she can't believe that anyone with a grain of intelligence would stand behind someone like her? She says she will "expose" me to my colleagues for not joining her in her Zen Buddhist dieting, and I make excuses for her. She talks about suing our neighbor because that woman is feeding her children marsh mellows instead of celery sticks and raw carrots, and I'm actually thinking of accompanying Ellen to the police station. How dumb can you be?

She is lecturing me now on the historic wrongdoings of the members of my gender and expects me to just swallow this. Not that I think she has nothing useful to say. I only wish she would differentiate, employ logic, or a least use a little common sense, use a brain, make use of all those synapses you normally develop at college. Where is her brain, Herr Doctor? You say you have looked inside her head. Mind over matter, isn't that your thing? So can you tell me, why should *I* take the blame for everything that's ailing her? Because I put the things she says in perspective? Because I hold a mirror in her face? Because I like to provoke her every now and then?

"I'm getting a bit tired now," I say before she has a chance to say something regarding my remark about men having a shorter life expectancy than women. "I think it's the jetlag. Maybe *you* want to drive for a while. What do you think?"

I say this nicely, in an accommodating tone of voice, and remember, I say this after she has spent the last half hour accusing me of not letting her drive. I try to think positive, I'm ready to use whatever psychobabble might do the trick. I don't say that she *must* drive, not even that she *should* drive. I say maybe, and I ask her what she thinks about my suggestion. I give her a choice, and I mean it. But her answer is like the bark of a pit bull charging at me. "What?! Me driving, now, with all these cars, in a foreign country? Do you want me to get killed? *You* are tired? What do you think *I* am? Do you think I slept on that plane?"

"I didn't sleep either," I answer in the softest voice I can muster at this moment.

"But you had the better seat. You had lots of space to move your elbows, while I had to sit next to the window, on the outside wall where it's cold. I can't sleep when I'm freezing."

Why are you looking at me like that? No, I did not force her to sit at the window. *She* insisted on getting the window seat. *She* was the one who told the lady at the check-in counter where she wanted to sit. And no, I did not remind her that she had the seat she requested. Is that strength of character, or is it cowardice that I was showing here? I was speechless, but I wouldn't have gotten a word in anyway. She went on and on about the flight having been delayed, about the airline not offering enough legroom, and about having gotten a raw deal when she agreed to come along on this trip. She also accused *you* of having talked her into this – because you are a man, I suppose.

"I didn't sleep a wink," she said. "I'm exhausted, my side hurts, I have the most awful jetlag, I can't see straight, and now you want *me* to drive. You are trying to kill me, I know!"

That was the point when I lost control, when I went ballistic, flew off the handle, and hit the ceiling. That's when I let out a scream. And a scream it was! I moved over to the right lane, I squeezed myself between two huge trucks, and I screamed bloody murder. I know people who would have called her names at this point, names like fruitcake, nutcase, or dingbat, or worse, shithead or scumbag. But not me, I have manners, I'm civilized. All I did was scream. I screamed so loud you could hear me in the cars passing us. I screamed for a whole minute, maybe two.

Now you might think a scream is nothing. I'm sure you've had your share of nutcases screaming in your office, or threatening to jump out the window, or sobbing for an hour, or whatever people do when they let off steam. For many people screaming is something they do naturally when they are in emotional pain and are lost for words. But to me, letting out this scream - maybe it was more of a long drawn-out howl - meant something else. I recovered my civil liberties, you see, not by putting forth rational arguments and using diplomatic language, but by screaming my lungs out. On the plane I had been quiet when she complained about me laying hands on her luggage and people were staring at me, and for the last half hour I had buried my fury in sarcasm, which is not my preferred way of articulating an opinion. In-between silence and sarcasm I had tried to reason with her, using a normal tone of voice, and I probably had blood on my lips from biting my tongue. But now I was at the end of my wits, and I screamed. God did I scream!

Dr. Birnbaum, I lost my temper, and this on the first day of this vacation. I am telling you this because for a minute or two I conducted myself in a way that is not me. My mother would disown me if she saw me behave like this, and my students would drop my courses if I screamed like that in the lecture hall. You'd think I was a character in a bad comedy. But this wasn't a comedy, and what happened during the next few days wasn't funny either. No surprise there. If there *was* a surprise, it was in the way I put an end to this madness, when I decided on a harsh but, I hope you agree, perfectly sensible course of action, when I faced the facts and did the "manly" thing.

This Gap Is Too Wide

The hotel in which we spent the first night was a three-star establishment on the outskirts of Baden-Baden. From the looks of it, it was a building erected sometime in the late 1950s to early 1960s, originally intended as a residence and turned into a fifteen-or-so-room hotel probably just a few years back. Nothing fancy, but perfectly okay for a couple exhausted from a six-hour drive to the airport in Toronto, a seven-hour flight to Germany, and then a further two hours driving on a busy motorway. The plan was to spend the afternoon and one night in Baden-Baden. We would explore this city a bit, maybe do some shopping, and, if she's up to it, spend a couple hours in the famous spa. I thought the hotel I picked would suit our purpose just fine, but when Ellen woke up the next morning I could tell from the tortured expression on her face that she was of a different opinion. No Bible in the drawer, no shower separate from the bathtub, no king-size or at least queensize bed, and no English-language television channel. "This hotel has none of the basic amenities I need when I'm so far from home," she would say, if I asked her if she had slept well.

And I didn't ask her if she was okay. For one thing, she wouldn't take this question seriously. She'd say it's pretty much routine to ask your spouse if she is okay. Everyone asks this question, and after you have been married for ten years it becomes a reflex after a while. It's something you say without thinking. She would also say that I have no right to ask this question, because I don't mean it. I'm not at all concerned about her well-being, because if I were, I would have gotten us a better hotel. And thirdly, I should not ask if she is okay when I know darn well that she is not okay, especially since I am the reason that she is not okay.

Having breakfast together that morning was an experience all by itself. If you want to understand what happened, it might help if you remember the session about a year ago when she changed chairs several times because she couldn't decide what was worse, sitting at the window and getting her face sunburned, or sitting across from you at your desk and staring at the bust of a grim-looking Freud. Decision-making has never been her strong point, but on that morning she was confronted with a whole new set of conditions.

So imagine this scene, if you are up to it. We enter the restaurant and she proceeds straight to one of the tables at the window, telling me on the way that after a terrible night like this she wants the morning sun to shine on her face. But as soon as we are sitting and she takes a look out the window she changes her mind. What she sees is not a park with fancy flowers and luscious trees, or some of those buildings with a baroque facade, where in previous times the international nobility used to lounge. What she sees is a paved parking lot. Because I had told her that Baden-Baden is a picturesque town, she has a right, she says, sounding like a five-year-old who insists on getting a patio addition for her dollhouse, to sit at a table with a "nice view."

I don't mind, so we move to a different table. She chooses - please note, *she* makes the selection - a table at a window to the side of the room. This time she has a view of a couple of cherry trees and some shrubbery. Things seem to be okay, but when she comes back from the buffet, where she had a first look at the offerings, she says that this section of the restaurant is too dark. Why would she have to sit at a table in an area that is dark and dingy, when the sun is up already? I say, no, we don't have to sit in the dark, let's change tables, no problem. If the sun is more important to you than a nice view out the window, we could go back to the table we had before. But this table is now taken, so we walk to the only other table available in the sunny section of the restaurant. But just before we get to that table, she protests: "Not *this* table. The sun is too bright here, I don't want to get a headache." The look she gives me says: Don't force me to sit there.

She scans the room for a few long, desperate seconds and then decides - note, *her* decision - to take one of the two free tables near the buffet. I follow her uncomplainingly. But once we are seated it doesn't take long before she tells me that this table is no good, that it's too close to the buffet, where it's too loud. "I can't stand the noise," she whines. "That commotion, I can't take this, my nerves are shot as it is." She looks with contempt at a family sitting not far from our table, with their two children running back and forth to the buffet, chasing each other, shrieking and giggling, and the parents not doing anything about this.

I use reason wherever I can, so I ask: "Shall we move?" "No, we just sat down," she says curtly. "But you said you can't stand that noise." "So why do *I* have to move? I am not the one making all this racket. *They* should move." "They are four people, with kids. It's easier for us to move to another table." "But I don't feel well." "They don't know that." "Then tell them." I don't want to make a scene, so I say: "Let's wait a bit, maybe they will tell their kids to be quiet." "You're kidding. Have you forgotten how it was with Chrissie?" "I'm just trying to be helpful." "Well, you are not. You are being asinine about this." "How is that, dear?" "Don't call me dear. I'm not your dear." "Okay, no dear then. Shall we go and have breakfast somewhere else?" "No! I don't want to argue with you."

At this point she notices a table in the far corner of the room. That's where she wants to sit, she says. This table fulfills all her criteria, I'm thinking. It's in a quiet area, far enough from the buffet, not quite in the sun, but certainly bright enough for us to see what's on our plate, and there are no unruly children nearby. The problem is that this table isn't set, so I ask the waitress if she would be so kind to set it for us. The expression on her face is a mixture of irritation and confusion. She wants to know why we keep changing tables. I have jetlag, I tell her, I slept only a few hours, so I'm a bit disoriented. So once again, I take the blame for Ellen's erratic behavior.

While I talk to the waitress, Ellen goes to the buffet. When she comes back to our table, I'm still busy with the waitress. I want her to think of us as an exhausted but otherwise normal couple. I'm afraid that her assessment of us changes when Ellen asks her, in simple English, if she could have a poached egg and two slices of whole-wheat toast. There is no whole-wheat bread on the buffet, she says, in the United States it is commonplace to have not just white bread on offer, but also whole-wheat bread and whole-grain cereals, things the human body needs to stay healthy. And while she is now giving the waitress a lecture on nutrition, she also mentions the milk problem. She had not seen any low-fat milk on the table, if the waitress could bring a bit of low-fat milk, with fat content not more than zero point one. The waitress shakes her head and mumbles, in English with a strong German accent: "Milk is milk, vee heef normaal milk." She looks at me with an expression that says something like, normal people drink normal milk. If I had any guts, I'd say to her: Just bring a couple slices of whole-wheat bread, and zer vil bee no mor trubl.

Of course, she has no idea what a poached egg is, so I explain it to her. She listens, but shows no great interest, and then she declines Ellen's request, saying that this sort of egg is not on the menu, but that they offer both hard and soft-boiled eggs. Oh, now you should hear Ellen. She may be tired and she may not feel well, but she has no problem letting this woman know the extent of her frustration. A three-star hotel in the States would have poached eggs on the menu, she says, not just standard hard and soft-boiled eggs, but also scrambled eggs, with and without ingredients, and fried eggs sunny side up or over easy. And if it's not on the menu, you can ask for it. In any good family restaurant in the States they make exceptions. A variety of egg menus should be standard also in Baden-Baden, which, her husband - she points a finger at me - had told her, is an international city. If she had dinner at this restaurant, would they also have only one type of potato on the menu, boiled or baked, or fried, or mashed? To conclude her tirade she points to the buffet and says that someone had just taken the last cucumber slices. "How long will it take for this tiny plate to be re-filled?" she demands to know.

I look around the room and I wonder if anybody near us had overheard this exchange. What would they be thinking? A woman on the edge because she has her period, or is she seriously ill? To be such an insignificant element in this vast universe and yet to think the world is made just for her. The couple two tables away from us shake their head at me in bewilderment. What patience that man has! Or rather, how stupid must he be to let her go on like this? You look at Ellen, how she is all over this poor waitress, and you get the impression she wants to take over that woman's business. You think she owns everything, commands over everybody, knows everything, and the future is hers alone. Nobody in this room knows what's going on with her, that she hits rock bottom every time she has a panic attack. If she knows anything inside out, it's the Bible. If she commands over anyone, it's me and our children - and her mother. And if the future is hers, it's a future of desolation.

The remainder of our breakfast together is out of this world too. Ellen goes back and forth to the buffet a number of times because she is unable to decide what to eat next and what kind of herbal tea she should try. And she changes chairs with me because she doesn't want to have that man sitting behind her. I'm looking around this room, thinking if I could just do what other people here are doing, reading the morning paper, spreading out a roadmap of the Black Forest, and planning with their partner the agenda for the day. I see a young couple holding hands across the table, an elderly man bringing his gratefully smiling wife a glass of juice from the buffet, and parents feeding their two-year-old pieces of a roll they dunk in hot chocolate. I'm thinking of our own children when they were toddlers. How Marcus would stand in his highchair and clap in excitement at the sight of his meal arriving, and how Chrissie would crawl into the kitchen to explore the world. A few years later I'm listening to Ellen going crazy over a plate of cucumbers that hasn't been re-filled yet, giving me a look that says, Don't just sit there and think you are going to have a relaxed breakfast, while I am stuck in this shithole of a hotel where they don't even have whole-wheat bread. Instead of defending me in front of this unfriendly waitress, who can't tell the difference between a boiled egg and a poached egg, you find nothing better to do than telling her you have jetlag. And don't think I haven't seen the eye that you gave her.

Now you must understand I have been watching Ellen for a good twenty minutes killing what under normal circumstances would be a peaceful breakfast on the first morning of a vacation. I willingly changed tables, I traded chairs with her without complaining, I translated the entire menu for her, and I apologized to the waitress. Other men would throw a glass of water in her face, but I am civil about all this. Even when I say to her, "You don't know what you want. Why don't you call your mother and ask her to tell you what you want?" I say it in a nice way.

Oh, you should see the look she gives me, like darts she's throwing at me. But is what I said really so different from what Dick said to Rosemary in "Tender is the Night", a line which the reader loves because Dick said it when he didn't know how else to deal with her advances? "You go and ask your mother what you want," it says in that novel. Ellen explodes, telling me I am condescending, I am not taking her seriously, I have no conscience, and I'm being negative. Normally she also says that I'm passive-aggressive. Not mentioning my passive-aggressiveness now, is that progress, Doctor, or just oversight?

She is so angry, she might as well be foaming at the mouth. People are now staring at us, the waitress is nowhere to be seen, and the couple at the table next to ours are leaving the restaurant, without finishing what's on their plate. One man has dropped his newspaper and is grinning at me. Another man is waving at me, and the woman sitting across from him is giving me a pained smile, as if to tell me that I should take a stand with Ellen. I imagine I look appallingly helpless, and I probably have "embarrassment" written all over my face.

You may remember what I suggested we do on this trip, that we spend a few days exploring parts of the Black Forest. We would drive around without any specific goal in mind. We would simply enjoy the landscape, stop in some of those quaint little towns hidden in deeply carved valleys, stroll around market squares, check out churches, maybe visit a heritage museum, most definitely see a cuckoo clock exhibit, and take walks off the road to have a look at some of those famous farm buildings with the huge wooden overhangs and flower-decorated balconies. After traveling around the Black Forest we would visit my mother for a few days. Ellen would then return home and I would stay in Southern Germany for another week to visit several city archives and museums, where I would pick up data and interview people for my research project. At the end of my stay I would attend a conference in Munich to present a paper. That was the plan, and you thought it was a sensible one.

I remember every word that was said in that meeting. She kept insisting "I don't know," but you told her to be "open-minded" about this trip. "No, I can't," she said. "Why not?" "He doesn't really want me to take a trip with him." "But *he* suggested that you come along. I heard him say it." "Yes, but you don't understand. He only thinks of his work, he never thinks of me, he doesn't care what *I* want." "But I heard him say that you could choose what to see and what to do." "That's what he said, but what he thinks is different." "What is he thinking?" "That he wants to combine this vacation with his work, so that he can save money." "But you said yourself that you need to save money." "Yes, but not when you are on a vacation. A vacation is different." "What's different about a vacation?" "This won't just be a vacation, it will be work, *his* work." "But he needs to do his job. He has research do to, and there is a conference he will attend." "You see, he goes there for work." "He said that he would do his work *after* you have gone home. The first week would be vacation, the second week he would be doing his work, while you are at home with your children and your parents. Do you remember that he said this?" "Yes, but what he says is not what he thinks. You don't know what he *really* thinks." "What *does* he think?" "That he would rather do his work than be with me. Don't you know this?" "I don't know what your husband is thinking, I only know what he said. He said he would be renting a car so that you would be free to visit places you want to see." "But I don't know what

I should see." "Then let yourself be surprised." "But I don't want to be surprised."

Doctor, I don't like surprises either. You said it would be good for her to be away from home, to be in a different environment for a while. I remember how you phrased it. The environment has a lot to do with our mood, you said. We spent the entire session going over this until she finally agreed, and now look what happened.

The Black Forest is indeed a very different environment from the places she has seen. As soon as you get out of Baden-Baden you think you are in a different world, with small towns that have their own unique history due to their geographic isolation before the development of industry. And the landscape is enticing too. It's calendar-art prettiness wherever you look, if the weather is good. And it *was* good. The sky was perfectly blue. It must have rained two or three days earlier, because the meadows looked incredibly rich, bathed in lush green sprinkled with bright yellow dots. When you stand on top of a hill and you look into the distance, you can see how expansive these thick forests really are.

When we left Baden-Baden that morning we took a road leading to one of the bigger towns, Freudenstadt, where we would arrive sometime in the afternoon, depending on the number of stops we'd make along the way. Our first stop was Eberstein Castle, a place with a history going back to the twelfth century. I suggested we sit in the garden restaurant outside the building facing south, assuming she would enjoy the view down the vineyard stretching all the way into Murgtal, the valley through which we would then drive to Freudenstadt.

First we went to the restroom. I was done before her, so rather than wait for her in the courtyard I went to the restaurant to pick out a table for us, a table under a big chestnut tree. While I waited for her, I looked through one of those visitor's brochures that I had found lying around in the courtyard. It contained pictures of the castle and featured a discussion of the apparently very painful history of this castle up to the nineteenth century, a history marred by battles over territory and religion. I will discuss this with Ellen, I said to myself, assuming she'd find it interesting to be in a place that had played an important role in the political and economic development of this region.

But when she finally showed up at the table, she had something very different on her mind. She said she had no interest hearing about "stupid kings and dukes," as she phrased it. There are far more important things to concern oneself with, she said, and when I asked her what these things were, she talked about the long waiting line outside the ladies' room. Wherever you go, not just in the States, but in Germany as well, as she just discovered, the designers of toilet facilities don't care to know that women have vastly different requirements than men. The reason why they don't care is that they are men. She had just stood in line with half a dozen other women, waiting to get into one of only two toilet stalls. Men have urinals in addition to stalls, so they can get on with life much faster than women. Getting on with life meant that they can enjoy themselves sitting in a restaurant and reading a newspaper or "stupid history brochures," while their wives wait in line for half an hour to go to the toilet. Unfair, outrageous, obscene, those were some of the words she used to characterize this abominable injustice done to women.

"So what am I supposed to do about this?" I asked, expecting that she will take this question as an opportunity to fire a couple rounds of incriminations and accusations against me.

"You could complain."

"Complain to whom?"

"How about talking to the owner of this place?"

"And say what?"

"What I just told you, that there are not enough toilets for women."

"Why don't *you* go and tell him?"

"I don't speak German. *You* do, so *you* go and tell him. Ask him if this is a Muslim country."

"Why should I ask *that*? We all know that this is a Christian country. Women don't get beaten here, at least not for religious reasons."

"Then why is it so difficult here for women to get access to even the most basic things like toilets? You'd think you are in an Islamic society here, where men get all the privileges. A perfect way to subdue women is to make them stand in line when they need to go to the toilet. That's what's happening here. They are so keen here printing all those tourist booklets with color pictures of armors, swords, and coats of arms, but when it comes to doing something really important, like providing more toilet facilities for women, they couldn't care less."

She was right, in a way, and what she complained about was nothing new to me. It was the fanaticism in the way she attacked me for something that was none of my doing, which I found so annoying.

"You get to sit here in peace," she said, "and you read about how the rich and powerful men here used to enlist starving peasants to protect their privileges, while I have to stand in line forever just to pee."

Of course it wouldn't be Ellen if she left it at that. She now started ranting about men winning all the prize money, and about dukes holding peasant daughters as slave girls to sweeten up their quiet hours. And when she was finally done with dukes and kings she returned to those wicked male engineers who deliberately misdesign women's toilets in order to degrade women. She mentioned Gloria Steinem and Betty Friedan because she thought they had an opinion about this toilet calamity too. She even quoted a couple lines from Virginia Woolf's work, on which she had written her eighty-two-page undergraduate thesis, plus sixteen pages of "works cited."

I didn't say anything, it wouldn't have done any good. It was only when she said something about Virginia Woolf that I knew was wrong that I corrected her. And I said it nicely, putting the blame on her thesis supervisor having overlooked something, a minor detail perhaps, but still something worth noting. Now she accused me of claiming that I knew more about Virginia Woolf than she did. She was almost hysterical at this point. She spoke so loudly that a group of American tourists walking by stopped listening to their tour guide. I suppose they found Ellen's lecture far more interesting than what their guide had to say about the history of the vineyard to my right. "Yes, ma'am, you're right, ma'am," I heard myself protesting in my head, as she lectured me on what Virginia Woolf had *really* said.

If you think she had run out of steam by the time we left Eberstein Castle, you are wrong. I had parked the car at a rest stop where I had seen a sign pointing to a hiking trail that takes you to a creek a couple hundred meters into the woods. I thought that going for a walk for half an hour or so would calm her down a bit. The idea of spending some time in this pristine forest at this time of the day, when the air from last night was still cool, seemed very inviting to me. Who wouldn't be blissfully happy in a place like this?

Well, Ellen was not happy. We had hardly reached the bottom of the ravine that she started complaining about her shoes, or rather about me for not telling her to wear different shoes. Mind you, what she wore were not wooden clogs or five-inch high heels. She wore regular loafers, maybe not perfect for this trail, but certainly okay for managing a few hundred meters on small gravel and dry leaves. Well, there was the occasional tree root sticking out of the ground, but she sounded as if she had been climbing over a pile of razor-sharp rocks. And when she saw those boulders in the river bed, she cried how dare I force her to go on this so-called nature walk, which was more like doing an obstacle course. She scared the last bird away with her yapping and yelling. "You are doing this on purpose. You knew exactly how far this would be."

"So did you. You saw the sign at the rest stop which said it would be three hundred meters to this ravine. I saw you reading it."

"But it didn't say that this trail is not paved."

"Hiking trails are rarely paved, my dear."

"Stop that with your 'dear.' It's condescending."

I apologized for being "so insensitive" and suggested that, since we were here now, we could sit on one of those boulders for a while and enjoy the warm sun shining into the ravine.

"I don't want to sit here just to get some sun," she protested. "I can do that at home. We have gorges too. And our forests are bigger than what you have here."

Doctor, believe me, I had no desire to quarrel with her about the expanse of forests in the Appalachian Mountains or the height of trees in the Adirondacks, or to argue about the depth of gorges in upstate New York. I just wanted to sit there for a few minutes and listen to the water trickling down the slope, maybe take off my shoes and socks and put my feet into the water. Goddammit, isn't that what normal people do everywhere in the world, when they stumble on to some water hole after a long hike through the woods?

Instead of enjoying the serenity of this place, we stood there arguing about the bad quality of women's shoes. I told her that my shoes weren't exactly hiking boots either, but this was no valid argument for her. Doctor, I'm not lying, she actually said that the men who design women's shoes design them *purposively* to hurt their feet. And she said this as if *I* work in the women shoe business and I took her on this trail to prove it. Is there a law I am breaking when I suggest we go on this walk? Is it my destiny to be accused of being so cunning that I trick her into this walk? Then she brought up an argument about high heels, using a somewhat different logic, but arriving at the same conclusion. High heels, she said, were a method to ensure that women can't run away from their husbands, similar to the tight-fitting clothes and tiny shoes that geishas used to wear, so that they could only patter around. Shoes were a method to uphold the tradition of men being kings, and women being geishas, she said. When I pointed out to her that women in the States nowadays wear sneakers even on city streets, she replied that they do this only on their way to the office. As soon as they sit at their desk they change into high heels, so they can look attractive for the men prancing around them all day. Well yes, there is truth to this. Men do like to be around women who wear high heels to show off their well-shaped legs, but does she have to get hysterical about this?

And then came her climactic argument, some concept that was meant to finish me off. Men force women to wear pumps even in bed, she said, and they certainly don't do this to make them feel comfortable. No joke, Doctor, we are standing in the middle of a virgin forest and she wants to discuss one of her "facts," the idea that men force women to wear shoes in bed. She went on and on about how degrading this is for women, how insulting, and how … well you can guess the rest. I tried to reason with her, saying jokingly that some of my colleagues ask their wives to wear flip-flops in bed, which would be more comfortable than wearing pumps. But she was in no mood for jokes. She blew up, and all life around us, all those bumblebees and butterflies criss-crossing the ravine, all that came to a sudden standstill.

Dr. Birnbaum, is what I said really so bad? Can't I even make a joke anymore? Sure, I could have been catatonic about all this, but she would have accused me of playing the I-don't-care-game. I was merely joking to relieve tension. But even if I had been serious, is the act of women wearing shoes to bed really a violation of their dignity? Can it not also be considered a natural part of coupling, people giving and taking sensuous pleasure? And tell me, is what she said to me, her fanatical yapping about men having no other goal in mind than to design women's shoes for extreme *discomfort*, is that something you would call a cognitive distortion, treatable with a simple talking cure, or is it something very serious, something requiring heavy medication or electric shock therapy? You might want to discuss that with her. Ask her what *she* wears to bed. No, it's not shoes. She has never worn shoes to bed, and believe me, that's no loss to me. She can wear whatever she wants to, she can wear snow boots to bed, for all I care. I'm finished with her as it is.

Oh, I'm so sick and tired of this megalomaniac theater of hers. For a split second I actually thought about leaving her in that ravine and running away. What if she got lost in the woods? How long would it take her to find back to the car and discover that I'm gone? What a story that would be for the local newspapers, with the headline: GERMAN HÄNSEL FORGETS AMERICAN GRETEL IN MURGTAL!

Well, I did not run away, as you can guess. I'd feel guilty, the shame would kill me on the spot. It's more likely that I would carry her back to the car, to avoid her accusing me of wanting her to scrape her delicate feet on some rock or trip over some root. I don't suppose you know the short story by an Italian writer, a story entitled "The Woman in the Saddle." It's a story about a man whose wife takes pleasure in putting a harness around his neck and then jumps on his back to have him carry her through the entire house. She treats him like a horse, apparently out of fear that he will leave her. He lets her abuse him like this because otherwise she would lie in bed all day, lamenting over whatever ails her, and not eating anything. I thought of this bizarre story on the way back to the car. Now do you want to analyze *this*?

She had more to complain about when we were back on the road, and it wasn't even lunchtime yet. The first thing that annoyed her was a huge trailer truck in front of us that I couldn't pass. It emitted so much pollution that at some point she asked me to pull over and stop the car. Now, this is where you come in. She said that you had told her to get as much fresh air as possible, that fresh air would help clear her head, so driving behind a diesel truck - and others, which I had been able to pass eventually - she considered an assault on her health. My answer, the idea that she could have stayed longer in that ravine, if she wanted fresh air, she called an insult to her intelligence. Being in that ravine for an entire day wouldn't change the fact - one more "fact" - that this road was "full of stinking diesel trucks," in a region that advertises itself as offering pure nature. Now, who can argue with that?

We finally stopped in a small town with the pretty name Klosterreichenbach. Try saying it: KLOSTER-REICHENBACH. Sounds melodic, doesn't it? And it has the word "cloister" in it. That alone should excite her. Maybe a brief walking tour in this tiny town would be good for her nerves, I thought. I suggested we might first look at the market square and then visit the church. Her shoes would be perfectly fine for walking on these streets. They were well-paved and there were no obstacles on the road that she might trip over or bump into. She didn't take lightly to those remarks which, I admit, were a bit cynical. But when I mentioned the monastery that I had come across in some travel guides, she brightened up immediately.

Thank God, the monastery church was open to visitors. She was ready to kneel and pray in no time, which was obvious from the way she rushed to the entrance. I was moved by this church too. You think you are not in this world: the stale air, the dank chill sinking into your bones, white-washed walls, and no furnishings other than plain benches. And hanging above the side entrance is a huge cross with a ten-foot tall Jesus figure on it. It's the first thing you notice when you stand at the main entrance. This symbol of suffering is so large and heavy that you have to be afraid it'll crash down on you when you think of yourself as a sinner and you slam the door shut.

By bringing Ellen to this magnificent site of holiness have I finally done something right? I see her shudder at the sight of this cross. What is she thinking? What Mark said in the primal Gospel, "What God has joined together, let not man put asunder?" Or what Paul said about the married couple, "They two shall be one flesh?" Or, more likely, is she praying to God to punish me for my "hardness of heart"? I remember what she said at breakfast, that I had given the waitress the eye, meaning I had shown interest in her. Maybe she is now reciting that biblical stuff about adultery, that I will eventually "put away my wife and marry another" and that I shall not be forgiven, should I ever lust after another woman, if I "see a woman fairer than she." You ask, how do I know these biblical phrases that are popping in my head one after the other? Well, that's easy, you live with Ellen for as long as I have, and you learn those phrases when you go to church with her, hear her talk to herself, and read some of those notes she has been distributing around the house for the last few months.

You know what I am talking about, right? Those notes, which are probably part of an assignment you gave her, to express her feelings by writing out what's tormenting her. That she spreads those notes all over the house may not be part of the assignment, but it shows how seriously she takes these things. Many of the words are crossed out and then rewritten, and then crossed out again. Tell me, does she think you will grade her writing? If you ask me, the stuff she writes there is silly but quite useful if you want to know something about the workout she gives her mind every now and then. You wonder what's up when you read three notes in one week that say that having sexual intercourse with your husband is a constitutional right, and in another note she complains that I don't want to learn anything about the sexuality of witches. How can she say this after I had just finished reading Updike's "Witches of Eastwick?"

Anyway, she stands at the front entrance of this church and stares at this huge cross over the side entrance. After a minute or so she walks down the aisle to the altar, kneels down, makes the cross, not once or twice, but half a dozen times, and then sits down on the bench in the first row. While she's praying – or at least that's what I think she is doing – I pick up a booklet from a stand near the entrance and go back outside to sit on a bench. The booklet gives an overview of the history of this monastery, founded in the eleventh century, governed variously by two factions of royalty – one of whom were also the rulers of the Eberstein Castle we had just visited – who fought for control until the Reformation, when it turned Protestant, was re-catholicized in the Thirty Years' War, and then became Protestant again after the Peace of Westphalia. So much fuss over religious correctness, and now it's just a plain church for tourists to get some relief from the hot sun outside.

When later that day I said to Ellen that this church looked rather barren to me, she protested wildly. I should keep my opinion to myself, she yelled. If she wanted to hear my opinion, she'd ask for it. Or write a note and place it under my pillow, I almost said out loud. If you want to be close to God, she said, you don't need decorations. I said, yes, it's like eating strawberries directly from the ground. To enjoy the taste of strawberries you don't need a bowl and a spoon.

Now you should have heard her. Comparing faith to eating strawberries is a sin, she said. I replied that I didn't question her belief in God, I just wanted to make the point that if you enjoy something, whether it be eating strawberries or reading a book, you don't need the surroundings in which you are enjoying that thing to be dressed up. You enjoy that thing because it's pleasant in itself. I was merely articulating my opinion about the interiors of this church, I said.

Before we left the monastery grounds I translated for her the information I had picked up in the booklet as well as the information provided on several display panels outside the church, which showed a map of the premises and explained graphically how the various buildings had developed over the last nine hundred years. She seemed impressed, although I wasn't sure if the reason for this was my high-quality translation or my showing interest in something that meant so much to her. Or maybe it was the peace of mind she had gotten from praying.

If it was peace of mind, it had evaporated by the time we arrived in Freudenstadt. She didn't like this city. I could tell as soon as we stepped out of the car that I parked on the market square, apparently the largest market square in Germany. She found this place "odd," saying it was "not right" having such a big open square with a church "tucked away in the corner." Actually, it's a huge and domineering building with two massive towers. Even a blind person can't miss it. There is no law that says that a church has to be in the center of town, I said to her, in a tone, she claimed, was insulting.

As we were walking across the square, I noticed that her facial muscles were twitching violently, you know, this convulsive jerking around the mouth when she is in serious disagreement with someone. What would she do if I took off now and left her standing here, I asked myself, watching her face break out in hives. Would she go to that church to pray, or would she look for the police station to press charges against me? Or would she sit down on one of those benches in this square, talking to herself, while waiting for me to return? I imagined that the people sitting nearby would look up from their newspaper to see what this person looks like who is stuttering to herself, and after a while they'd get up and leave. Everyone around her would sense that something is wrong with her. You can smell it against the wind, they'd say.

And you know, this is something quite a few people actually *did* say to me when they first met her, many years ago, after I had just moved in with her. Something is not right with her, they said to me, but I didn't listen. I didn't pay attention when they talked about what I might be getting myself into if I continued hanging around with her. And I didn't just hang around with her. For God's sake I *married* her. Was I simply too young, at thirty still the impetuous adolescent, unable to pick up on the vibes she was emitting even then? Or do I have a special weakness for "complicated" women, that curious mix of traits indicating a combative and damaged personality? Or was I just plain stupid? Could I not distinguish between self-assured women who feel strong when they are on their own, and needy women who are in distress when they are alone, thinking I fell for the former, when in fact I got the latter? Just a few days before we married, her mother said to me that her daughter was "different."

For some reason I didn't ask her what she meant by this, but believe me, if she were here now, I would say a thing or two to her.

Well, I didn't run away, leaving her in Freudenstadt so she can enjoy this city by herself. Sorry for the pun. Freudenstadt means "City of joy". We drove to Schiltach, an old, meticulously restored town near the center of the Black Forest. Standing at a lookout on top of one of the surrounding hills, you'd think you are looking at a movie set for the filming of Rapunzel. What you see is a small-town creation of great aesthetic thoughtfulness, timber-frame architecture wherever you look, and two long narrow streets meeting in the market square like the handles of a dowsing rod. I imagined how in the late Middle Ages people would walk down these streets every day to meet in the market square, where they exchanged commodities of all sorts, traded money and stories, and for entertainment watched performances of jugglers, singers, and puppeteers.

That this is not a town that takes heritage lightly you realize when you explore some of those narrow alleyways. I pointed out to Ellen the decorative plates and signboards on buildings, indicating the particular trade that was practiced there many years ago. I also showed her the numbers painted on some of the buildings, written in gothic style and telling the year when the building was erected, numbers like fifteen-hundred ninety-one or sixteen-hundred thirteen. I thought she would appreciate all the work that had gone into restoration to celebrate the history of this town. But she didn't care about architecture or symbols of medieval workmanship. I could tell from her flushed cheeks that her mind was on something other than the question how much history can be packed into a hundred meters of street. She didn't say much other than that she was tired of walking on cobblestone and that she didn't care if cobblestone streets gave me the feeling that this town came right out of a fairy tale, something I had said earlier.

I had taken her to this town because I hoped she would find here something that would be of academic interest to her. You would think that someone with a liberal arts degree has an interest in historical matters, right? Besides, there is someone in her family who, three or four generations ago, had come from the northern part of Switzerland, which is close to the Black Forest. So I thought she would have an interest in learning something about the history of this region, rather than merely driving around and looking at the landscape. Also, I was desperate to discuss something intellectually more stimulating than shoes or toilets.

She agreed that we sit in a restaurant on one side of the market square for a while, at a table outside. I wanted to talk about the market square as an institution in the late Middle Ages, but she didn't pay any attention. She just sat there, staring at a group of Asian tourists who stood around the fountain not far from us, listening to what their tour guide was saying. It was only when this lady pointed to the town hall a few meters up the slope that Ellen asked me to translate the inscriptions on the murals on the facade of this building. The paintings showed a picture of a fierce-looking duke who ruled Schiltach in the mid-fifteen century. They also represented some of the guilds that were at the center of economic life at that time, and the inscriptions on the murals included words like duty, honor, and commitment. Ellen asked me if duty meant duty to God or duty to the family. I replied that I didn't know, but probably it meant duty to a king or a duke, possibly also to the church, at which point she stood up and walked up to that building to study the murals up close. When she returned she was furious. "There are no women in these pictures," she said. "The only woman shown is the woman in that painting on the left. She's the person holding a torch, and the devil is grabbing her from behind. I bet she's the woman they accused of having laid the fire."

The mural she talked about suggested that there had been devastating fires in the years 1510, 1533, and 1590. I was honest and I said that I had not noticed that the only woman shown in those murals was a person doing something wicked, and that I had no explanation why the artist wouldn't show women participating in the life of this town in positive and important ways. I said that people in the institutions of small towns in rural regions in Germany sometimes make decisions not quite in line with what you would expect in a modern society. I used words like oversight, error, and ignorance, something you find even in expensive restoration work, and then she erupted with rage, yelling at me as if *I* had commissioned the work on these paintings: "What do you mean, restoration? What kind of restoration is that when they ignore the people who did the *real* work? You call that oversight?! I call it oppression, the same kind of oppression that goes on in a patriarchal society where women do all the work, but they keep them locked up in the house and then they don't even mention them in public displays that are supposed to show what life was like in this place. And when they do show a woman in those paintings, she's the person doing something evil. She is made responsible for fires, the pestilence, and God knows what else." She looked at the tourists in front of us and shouted, as if she wanted to teach *them* a lesson too: "Because she's driven by the devil! The devil is in the woman, that's the message in this picture. Do you know when they painted this? Before women got the vote? I don't want to sit here and look at this any longer."

The look she gave me at this point said: Do something about this. I answered: "You are absolutely right, but what do you want me to do? Do you want me to find out the name of the artist of these murals, or shall I have a word with the individuals in the town council who commissioned this work?"

I don't remember the exact words she used in her answer. It was something about me not wanting to face the fact. Oh, these facts! The fact that women don't count in these towns, that they haven't counted in the fifteen hundreds and that they still don't count, and that the public authorities in this country restore old towns so that they look like fairy tale places, rather than bringing them up to date politically, socially, and culturally. Doctor, I'm being castigated for something I'm definitely not responsible for. Honestly, I had wanted to show her late medieval architecture and talk about history, rather than wonder about the origins of some painting on the town hall. I suggested we leave, as it was getting late anyway, and we start looking for a hotel in some other town. To get back to our car we took a route that included a few detours, but at least the streets were paved and there were no murals in sight.

Good God, what terrible crime I had committed, taking her to a town full of cobblestone streets, knowing since our walk into that ravine this morning that she had a problem with her shoes. And it had been a terrible mistake to draw her attention to those murals before I had checked them out myself. Ellen had a point of course. You don't have to read Virginia Woolf to agree that women are at least as productive and ingenious as men. Without their work in the household the seas that men explored "would be unsailed and those fertile lands a desert," she wrote. If I did have a chance to talk to the commissioner of those murals, I would point out to him or her what an astute observer, male or female, might find repulsive in these displays. I would suggest adding a mural that shows the devil embracing the duke, a man who most likely had not been an active supporter of the local peasantry or of women's rights.

I was thinking about all this while driving down the road - again, we were stuck behind a truck for a while, and she gasped for air like a non-swimmer about to drown - until we reached a town called Bad Rippoldsau, which actually is an agglomeration of several tiny communities. She agreed that we should look for a hotel to stay for the night. It should be a *decent* hotel, she said and explained what she meant by "decent." She wanted a quiet place, not too close to the road, but not too far from the road either, that is, not a place hidden somewhere in the woods where she would feel depressed. There also had to be a "nice" view from the window, and the building must not have more than three floors. Why she considered three floors the limit was beyond me, and I didn't dare ask. She'd probably say that I should know her reasoning, I had been living with her for fifteen years, and if I were sensitive to her needs, I'd understand.

Her preferences were not so tight that I would have a problem finding accommodation for her, but I was wrong. She kept adding criteria as we looked at a number of hotels. The first hotel we drove up to was about four hundred meters away from the main road. There were only a few farm houses in the neighborhood, so it would be quiet there. And because it was located on a fairly steep hillside, I expected most rooms to offer a view of the valley. I had the receptionist take us up to a room on the second floor. When she opened the door and handed me the key, assuming the room was okay with us, I could tell immediately that Ellen had a problem. She walked to the window, pulled back the curtain and asked the lady in simple German if this was east she was looking to. The lady confirmed and Ellen said to me, in English: "No! Tell her that I can't wake up to the morning sun. This curtain is much too thin and it doesn't close right."

If this lady had understood English Ellen would now explain to her why she can't handle sunlight when waking up. But she didn't speak English, so it was my job to come up with a reasonable explanation. I didn't say that Ellen "has bad nerves" or that "she doesn't know what she wants." What I said, apologetically, was that my wife had been sleeping in rooms with windows to the west ever since she was a child. She was used to this, like other people are used to sleeping on one particular side of the bed. The lady said that the only other room available was one looking north. I apologized again, saying that my wife would feel closed-in in a room facing north, and a view up a hill this close would make it unbearable.

We then drove to another part of Bad Rippoldsau. The hotel I found did have a room that met Ellen's criteria, a quiet room not looking east, but south, in a two-storey building, if you don't count the attic, but she didn't like the furniture. The cupboard and the bedframe were too dark and too heavy-looking, which made this room depressing, she said. Also, she could smell cigarettes, in the furniture, in the bed sheets, and in the curtains. I could smell it too. I explained to her that the smell was a leftover from a time when people smoked in hotels and restaurants, even in cinemas and trains. We could keep the window open, I suggested. "No," she hissed, "I don't want to stay here. Or do you want me to get sick?" This was a clear warning to me: Find me another hotel or I will have a panic attack. You know my problem with that right? I returned the key to the lady at reception, and we left.

The next hotel we visited was one whose owner confirmed that the room was smoke-free. It offered an unobstructed, west-oriented view of the village and the hills on the other side of the valley. And it is definitely quiet, he promised. I signed the register, while he handed Ellen the keys and explained to her, in fairly good English, that one of the keys was to the front door of the building, so we would be free to enter the hotel late at night, if we wanted to go for a stroll in town. We then went upstairs, past two-feet tall statues of Holy Mary and I-don't-know-which-saint, on which Ellen commented very favorably. So I thought, great, we can stay here. When we then entered the room she did indeed express satisfaction with what she saw. I went down to the car to get our suitcases, and when I came back to the room I saw her sitting on the bed, leaning over to the middle and running her hand down the gap between the two mattresses. Without looking at me, she let out a shriek: "I can't sleep with a gap like that!"

I was stunned. "But it's just an inch."

"No!"

"We could stuff towels into the gap."

"But then there is a hump."

"Are you saying you can't sleep because of a hump?"

"Yes, a hump is as bad as a gap."

"But if you use a towel, it would be a *soft* hump."

"I'm not having this discussion with you. I don't want to sleep in a bed with a gap like this. Why can't you just accept that?" She looked at me as if *I* was out of my mind. "I want you to find another hotel."

Now, *you* may know what went on in that head of hers. I would guess it had something to do with her thinking in absolutes. It doesn't matter if it's a gap, a hump, a board, or barbed wire, there must be no obstacle between us, period. Maybe it's superstition that's driving her. It's a sign from God, two mattresses and a gap, and the marriage is over. She might as well sleep in the attic, and me in the basement. I think I spent a full ten minutes explaining to this man that everything was perfect, the size of the room, the way the furniture was arranged, and also the phenomenal view out of the window. I said that my wife liked his hotel, especially the staircase with those big statues symbolizing good values. The problem, really the *only* problem, I said, was the gap between the mattresses. You don't know how stupid I felt saying this: "My wife is American and she has a problem with the gap between the mattresses." He looked baffled, so I explained: "Americans normally sleep on a single, broad mattress because they want to feel like kings or queens, just like Germans who like to feel French sleep on a French bed." I don't know if he took this as a joke or as an offense, but just in case he thought I was pulling his leg, I said that I would recommend his hotel to a colleague of mine in the States who was planning a vacation in the Black Forest next year.

I then drove back to the part of Bad Rippoldsau where we had begun our search for a hotel an hour ago. I circled through the village a few times, until I located a hotel that seemed worth looking at more closely. The owner I spoke with was a very attractive lady, but given her age of around fifty, Ellen wouldn't think of her as competition, so I felt safe to give her a few smiles. Her English was only rudimentary, but she maintained eye contact with both of us, and when she talked with me, it was as if she addressed both of us. She went to great lengths to explain that this hotel was located in a very quiet part of the village, that she could offer breakfast as early as six-thirty, if we wanted to get on the road early, that the breakfast menu included homemade marmalade, honey from local beekeepers, and fresh rolls from a bakery next next door. Tomorrow would be another sunny day and the famous spa, where Rainer Maria Rilke had been a guest, was not far from here. There were a few other things she mentioned which, she promised, would make this a most pleasant stay for us.

"The room is okay", Ellen said, as we stood at the door peeking in. I was about to walk over to the bed to check the gap between the mattresses, when she discovered the small crucifix hanging above the headboard. "It's good to have Jesus Christ with us in the room, but I think it should hang over there," she said, pointing to the wall opposite the bed. "You should be able to see the cross when you lie in bed." I translated this as accurately as possible, adding the explanation that Ellen came from a deeply Christian family, where certain artefacts carry much symbolic value. As if to confirm what I just said, Ellen walked over to the wall facing the bed and placed her finger on a spot just above eye level. "Here, this is the best place." The lady of the house looked at me as if to say: What's wrong with you that you let her be this way?

Good question. Is it my talent for demonstrating empathy for the insane, while I'm vomiting my brains out? Practicing self-restraint even in the most ridiculous situation, is this my daily bread? If that is my problem and you think it's cutting into my own mental health, we should talk about this. I let it go because I thought, if I don't, the upcoming night will turn into a nightmare for me. She'll start an argument that will run all night and then, sometime around three or four in the morning, it will end with another one of her panic attacks.

Don't tell me I should be used to this, getting up in the middle of the night, packing up our children, and running the whole family to the hospital, just to have some doctor say to me, "Don't worry, Professor, everything will be okay." Here in this tiny town in the middle of the Black Forest, a panic attack would have an entirely new quality. I am stranded in a foreign country, pretty much in the woods, you could say, with no hospital nearby, and no doctor who knows enough of her history to take one quick look at her and say, "Don't worry, things are okay." You sent her on this outing with me, telling me it would be okay, but obviously it's *not* okay. If you could just see our saintly lieutenant, overbrimming with self-conviction and insisting that she knows exactly where the crucifix must hang to give the guests of this hotel some peace of mind. Believe me, if there had been a doctor in the house, I would have giving him your number, so *you* could talk to him.

It was past six o'clock now and getting too late to look for another hotel she might find agreeable. I suggested to Ellen that this hotel may not be perfect, but at least there was a holy cross in the room, which she could see as a major advantage over the other hotels we had looked at. But instead of listening to me she spoke to the lady, in English, with a few German words thrown in here and there, saying that there were good reasons for positioning the holy cross opposite from the bed. She went into considerable detail with this issue, and I translated, as required. The holy cross should be positioned in such a way that one can communicate easily with God through His son. "It's all so simple," she said. "God says that those of you who forgo sleep to be with your Creator, those whose faces stare up at me, you will see me in your hearts." I thought about asking her, if that is so, if we see in our heart, would it then matter where the holy cross is positioned?

I didn't ask her. Instead, pointing to the window I said to Ellen that this was a very nice-looking church out there and that it was close enough to walk there in the morning. It was a Catholic church, I added – the lady behind me nodded vigorously –, so the bells would ring very early in the morning, which would be better than having bright sunlight wake her up. "It's a very pretty church. It's not just some barren nave with a spire on top, but a masterpiece of human ingenuity, with an altar and a golden tabernacle that is mentioned in just about every guide to churches in the Black Forest." Ellen hesitated, so I added: "They say this church is God's work. We could visit it in the morning, if you want."

So this is how I got Ellen to stay at this hotel. Empathy on the outside, cunning on the inside, the rest was clever self-restraint. You just need to say the right words. Words like "God's work" and "worship in the forest" will do it. I managed to create a situation where we both spent a restful night, Ellen relaxing right underneath the holy cross, and me sleeping well *despite* this cross hanging over my head. I think she didn't even notice that there was a two-inch gap between the mattresses.

Back and Forth, Left or Right

You have to agree, forcing me to drive her from one hotel to the next so that she can get a room with the right view, a crucifix hanging on the right wall, and a bed with no gap between the mattresses, was sheer abuse. Or what else can you call this? Terror, torture, a crime against humanity? Someone less patient - or less deluded? - than myself would have reported her to Human Rights Watch. Still, this was nothing compared to what she did the following day, something that, if it were Mental Health Awareness Week, you'd consider a definite highlight. A naive outsider watching the two of us might think of this as a comedy, with Ellen playing the lead character and me being the fool, paralyzed by her behavior for which some people get locked away.

The day began quite well. Breakfast was peaceful, there were no arguments of any sort, and she didn't pester the waitress about anything. She was content with the way the boiled egg was done, the cucumbers were freshly cut, and the bread basket had dark bread in it, which she declared was wholegrain, although I'm sure it wasn't. On the downside, the church I had suggested we could have a look at was closed to visitors, because a television crew was setting up equipment for filming. But to my surprise, she didn't complain all that much about this missed opportunity and agreed that we drive straight to Hornberg.

Hornberg is famous for an event in the sixteenth century that historians still quarrel about if it actually occurred. In Germany, this "shooting" event is the source of a phrase that is used when people say that something important is going to happen, but then it doesn't. Famous literary figures like Friedrich Schiller and Thomas Mann referred to it, and Hannah Arendt mentioned it in one of her studies, when she wrote that a tense political situation may end in a revolution, or a counter-revolution, or, "as in the shooting at Hornberg," nothing may happen at all. Come to think of it, I could use this phrase on Ellen, when she keeps talking about getting a panic attack any moment, but it doesn't happen, or when it does, some doctor tells me it's nothing to worry about.

As we reached the outskirts of Hornberg and I saw the castle ahead of us – actually, it's a bunch of ruins perched on a rocky hill –, I thought about the possibility of having been here as a child. This town looked familiar to me, that oddly shaped hill, that imposing viaduct railroad bridge. When I made some remark to Ellen to the effect that I thought I had been here as a child, she wanted to know if being here now made me feel like a child? Which wouldn't surprise her, she said, as I behaved like a child so often. Or did I wish my father were here with us? She said all this as if it were some psychological abnormality to remember something good from childhood. She might have been thinking about her own childhood, or maybe she was nervous about seeing my mother the following day.

When we were having lunch in the garden restaurant of a hotel located right next to the castle, she brought up my father again. This time it had to do with that man sitting at the table next to ours. He was smoking a cigar and the wind kept blowing the stench right into our face. I would have suggested that we move to another table, but all tables shaded by trees were taken. When the dog of that man came over to our table to sniff at Ellen's leg, she started complaining, not to that man, but to *me* for God's sake. It was a long and emphatic declaration of her feeling assaulted, complete with the instruction for me to do something about this man. I didn't say anything to him, because he didn't look like a person who would apologize and recall his dog. And kicking this dog in the nose wasn't an option either.

My father had been a cigar smoker too, so I think this was the reason why she brought him up now. She talked about an incident that happened many years ago when he drove her to some store. I had not been witness to this incident, but she told me this story a number of times and in sufficient detail to know that she was seriously annoyed with him. He had not stopped the car for a woman with a stroller trying to cross the street – mind you, this woman did not stand at a designated pedestrian crossing. By not letting her cross the street he abused and degraded her, she said. Just what he did to Ellen when he never invited her to sit in the front seat when we were all in his car, my mother, myself, and Ellen. She said it should be basic courtesy for him to ask his daughter-in-law who is visiting him if she wanted to sit up front. It was as if he had refused to dance with her at her debutante ball.

Do you want to know what all these things have in common, my father not asking her if she wanted to sit in the front seat of his car, him not stopping for that woman wanting to cross the street, and the man in this restaurant not caring whether his loose-running dog and his smoking might be a nuisance to others? You see, she is convinced that she was put on this earth to save everyone from their own demise. And regarding my position in particular, she sees her mission in life as getting me to improve my understanding of the world, preferably *her* world.

You might keep this in mind when you hear about what happened an hour later, when we were back on the road and we came to a fork and a decision had to be made which way to go. She tried very hard to get me to understand her view of things, when in fact she was the one who didn't know what she wanted. At this fork you have the choice of going straight toward the Rhine valley or going north up a steep hill, following a sign suggesting that the traveler will have a breathtaking view of the surroundings. If you go straight, you will eventually reach a town known for its rich history in religious matters. There used to be many sites of religious significance, including cloisters, chapels, and prayer halls. All have been destroyed over the centuries, for reasons having to do with bishops and royalties wanting to replace old with new, a number of major fires, and willful as well as accidental destruction in the wake of the Thirty Years' War. Only the outer walls of an abbey are still standing today. I explained all this to Ellen as we got closer to the fork and then asked her which way she would like to go. Abbey road or scenic road? "I don't care," she said, "you decide."

I am telling you what happened now from memory. I'll do my best to be accurate, and where possible I'll quote what was said. There is nothing in this story that I am fabricating in order to impress you, annoy you, amuse you, or whatever. I am remembering this as if it were real-time, and I am not reconstructing it with reference to anything that has happened since then. I say this because if you don't know what a drama is, well, this was a drama, a *terrifying* drama, anguish of the highest order, with a heavy dose of insanity on the part of the protagonist. A drama for her, and a seminal moment for me.

I ask her a second time which road I should take. She'll make me bleed if I make a mistake. "I don't know, you decide," she says without hesitating.

"Are you sure?" I ask.

"Yes," she replies.

"Really?" I need to be absolutely certain.

"Yes. Just go."

I turn north because the sign says that this road offers something extraordinary. I expect a view of the Swiss Alps in the distance, the sky is perfectly clear, so I think taking this road is a good choice.

I am wrong. After not even five miles traveling up the hill she says icily: "I want to go the other way."

"But you said you wanted to go this way."

"*You* wanted to go this way, not me."

"You said that I should decide."

"That was then. I want you to turn around."

I figure we are not in a rush, so let her have her wish. I turn around and when I get to the fork, I stop and look at her. She doesn't say anything, she just stares ahead. I make a right turn. She still doesn't say anything, but after a few miles she puts her hand on my arm and says: "I want to go back."

"You mean, back to where we came from this morning?"

"No. I want you to go the other way."

"Going north again, up that hill? Why?"

"That road was more interesting."

"But I thought you wanted to go now to that town and look at the abbey there."

"I didn't say that. *You* wanted to see that place."

She is correct in that she had said nothing to my suggestion that we *might* visit that town, but she is wrong in her assumption that I *want* to see that place. Do you see the difference, Doctor? Might versus want. Inside I'm boiling, but the better side of me gets the upper hand. I think I am understanding and compassionate, and the splendid landscape with the luscious meadow to my left and the clear blue sky above me are of great help to me when I say to her: "Okay, let's go the scenic road again. But are you sure that's what you want?"

She hesitates for a few seconds and then says loud and clearly: "Yes."

I turn the car around and drive back to the fork, where I turn left, up the hill. After a couple miles she suddenly puts her hand on the steering wheel, grabbing it firmly and wiggling it, as if she wants to run us off the road and down the slope, shouting: "No, stop, I don't want to go any further."

My first task is to bring the car to a halt, which isn't easy with Ellen not letting go of the steering wheel. After a few meters the shoulder is wide enough to pull over and stop. Now that the car is no longer moving you'd think I explode, scream at her, or slam my fist on the dashboard, but somehow, and this is really a miracle, I remain calm, and without turning off the engine I say to her: "You know what? I think *you* should drive."

Without waiting for an answer I get out of the car, walk around to her side and open the door for her. To my surprise, she gets into the driver seat, not saying a word. But if you think she will turn the car around to go back, you are wrong. She drives in the direction that just a minute ago she said she did *not* want to go. But then, after a few miles she suddenly turns the car around and drives back to the fork and stops. I can see that she is struggling with herself, trying to decide which direction to go. She looks left, then right, then left again. She does this a few times, until she finally puts the blinker on left, but turns right, in the direction we had traveled before. I don't dare to ask if she plans to see that abbey now, or something else in that town, or simply pass through town. After a few miles, she turns around and drives back to the fork, but this time she keeps going straight, not saying a word. I am silent as well. I figure, she has taken ownership of driving, so let her be. We haven't gone very far, when suddenly she pulls over to the shoulder and stops the car, leaving the engine running. "You should have told me where these roads go to," she says, close to sobbing. "You should have helped me, instead of forcing me to drive."

"I did not *force* you to do anything," I reply, wondering if it's possible that I had said something, or had used a particular tone of voice, or had made some gesture that one could reasonably interpret as coercion.

"Yes, you did. You knew exactly that I wouldn't find my way around here. You have been here before, I haven't. And you put me on the wrong track on purpose so that I would get lost."

Lady, you are lost as it is, I am thinking to myself, but what I *say* is: "Sorry, Ellen, you *insisted* on driving. And you did not ask me for any advice. You wanted to drive, so I let you drive. Which is fine with me, no problem. You are free to drive."

I'm not trying to sound facetious, or condescending, or cynical. I want to appear lighthearted about all this, expecting that she'll yell at me now. But nothing happens, no word on her part. Just like the "shooting at Hornberg," I'm thinking. She turns around and drives back to the spot where she had turned around ten minutes ago and stares ahead for two or three minutes. Finally she turns off the engine and shouts: "This is not a vacation. You knew that this would happen, and so did Birnbaum."

"That's not true. It was Birnbaum who suggested that you go on this trip with me."

"No, *he* decided this, you *both* decided this. You didn't give me a choice. You are driving me crazy, both of you. You want to get me into the psych ward again. You want to get rid of me."

What do you do when she spews nonsense like that? I imagine I'm in the middle of a yoga session, killing thoughts I don't want to have. I answer softly: "No, Ellen, no one wants to put you away."

"Yes you do. But this time it will cost you dearly, I swear. This time it won't be just electroshock."

Without a word of explanation she gets out of the car and proceeds to walk across the street, not looking if a car is coming. For a moment I am thinking, no, I don't want her to disappear in the psych ward, but how would it be if she were killed by a car right now? And, forgive me, I'm thinking of your standard question: How does this make you feel? Yes, how *do* I feel? Afraid, relieved, elated? Ashamed even thinking about the possibility of her getting run over by a car, killed by her own stupidity? And how would I tell Marcus and Chrissi? You know your mother, she was somewhere else with her head when she crossed the road.

I watch her as she slowly crosses the street and walks into a freshly mowed meadow. She keeps on walking until she reaches a creek about a hundred meters from where I am. She sits down on something that looks like a tree stump. I don't know if she is crying, or screaming, or just staring into the water. To be honest, I don't care what she is doing or thinking this minute. After a couple of minutes she gets up and walks along the creek a few meters back and forth. She does this several times. Does she want to throw herself into the water to scrape her face on some sharp rock or to break a bone? I'm asking myself, is breaking an arm or a leg better or worse, from a psychological perspective, than having a nervous breakdown? But she doesn't go into the water, nor does she throw herself on the ground and crawl around on all four, as she did years ago in my parents' house, when she fell apart. Instead, she walks back to the street and then, after looking twice in both directions, crosses it quickly. Apparently, she has no intention of killing herself. No sooner has she reached the car than she screams at me, her face distorted with rage: "I can't do this! You have known this!"

"What do you mean, know *what*?" I really have no idea what she is talking about.

"You tricked me. You got me to go to this stupid country so that I would have a nervous breakdown. You want me to perish here."

"No, no, you won't have a nervous breakdown. You are on vacation. People don't have a nervous breakdown while on vacation."

"You call *this* vacation?"

"What do *you* want to call this then? A diving expedition, a field trip to never-never land, a picnic in the park, time-out in a circus?" Doctor, at this point I am having immense difficulty restraining myself. "Just tell me what you want. You have all the freedom in the world. You said you wanted to be without the children, so we left them at your parents' place. You wanted to drive this car, so you did. You wanted to go left, so you did. Then you wanted to turn right, so you did. Which way do you want to go now? Tell me."

She hesitates and then says: "But I don't know which is the better way to go."

"Then do you want to take a walk in the woods over there, or go for a swim somewhere around here? Or look at a church? What do you want to do?"

"I want *you* to drive."

"You want *me* to drive? And *where* do you want me to drive to?" I say this very slowly and I try to be gentle in the way I speak. I know, I should ask her to repeat what she just said, to get her to take full ownership of her words, but I'm afraid this would provoke another outburst of anger.

"I don't care. Go wherever you want to go."

What you normally do in a situation of complete uncertainty is you continue on the path you are on. So I decide to go in the direction *she* went before she stopped the car. But as soon as we are back on the road, she yells at me: "Had you told me you are going this way, I could have driven myself."

"You just said that you don't care which way I go."

"No, of course I care. You should have told me which way you are going, then I could have said something."

"Well, then please tell me now where you want me to go. Or do *you* want to drive again?"

"Oh, do whatever you like. You do this anyway. You always get *your* way."

Do you remember that I said there was a seminal moment during this trip when something happened, when things crashed? Well, this was that moment. I couldn't take it any longer, her lunacy, her morbidity, that torment of indecision, and on top of that my god-damn patience. Doctor, at that fork she was absolutely and certifiably mad. I didn't have it in me to slap her in the face, or vomit at her feet, and I couldn't just run away either. The decision I now made was not a solution. I knew that, but in my despair I couldn't think of anything else to do. I suggested we go to my mother's house a day earlier than planned. As if my mother, out of all people, would rescue me! But there was no benefit in spending another day driving around the Black Forest. I wanted to get away from this godforsaken place, not knowing that at my mother's house I'd be facing the next seminal moment. Or let's call it the second act of that moment – actually, it's the third act, because there is another once coming up first.

Strange enough, Ellen voiced no objection, so I drove back to Freudenstadt, where I looked for the shortest route to the Autobahn that would take us to Freising. Not far from Freudenstadt, where the landscape changes from thick forests and deep valleys to open fields and rolling hills, she suddenly grabs my arm and says that she wants to stay in the Black Forest for one more day. After all, this had been the original plan. One shouldn't change one's mind all the time, she says, if you can believe this. Besides, my mother wouldn't appreciate a change of plan on such short notice. Well, she got a point there, but since we are not far from Calw now, the town where Hermann Hesse grew up, I suggest we could stop there for an hour and then return to the Black Forest. We could look at some of the buildings and streets that are mentioned in his novels, I say to her.

A short while later, as we are driving through Altensteig, a small town not far from Calw, she says she is not feeling all that well. I suggest that we park the car somewhere near the river, where it's cooler, and look for a bistro. Altensteig is a medieval town with a very interesting looking old section perched on the side of a steep hill, with a castle on top and a church standing right next to it. Once you feel better we might have a look at the old town, I say to her. She agrees and as we walk down the main street, looking for a bistro, she notices a shoe store and immediately decides that she wants to buy a new pair of shoes. I remember the fight she had put up on our walk through the woods yesterday, and I'm thinking about the sightseeing drama on those cobblestone streets in Schiltach, so I can see why she wants to buy shoes now.

It takes her half an hour to find a pair of shoes she likes, for easier walking, she says to the sales lady, who is ostensibly pleased to have a customer from overseas in her store. By the time we leave the store she feels better, she tells me, but the moment we reach the car, where she wants to put on the new shoes, she decides that they are not the right shoes. "I don't want these shoes," she says, meaning we should go back to the store and return the shoes.

"But in the store you said that you like them."

"Yes, for walking, but I wanted a light color, something beige."

"So why did you buy them?"

"I couldn't see that they are dark brown. The light in that store wasn't bright enough." She looks at me as if I had instructed the store manager to dim the lights.

"You could have stood at the window and look at them there," I say, working hard to appear calm.

She hesitates a few seconds, probably thinking about the logic of my objection, and then says: "You would have talked me out of buying the other shoes I had tried on."

"How do you know?"

"Because you laughed at those other shoes."

"I laughed because these shoes would have made you look like a parrot."

"And that's why I shouldn't have listened to you."

"But you asked for my opinion."

"Only about the style, not the color."

So this is act II of the seminal moment on this trip. Maybe I'm deluded thinking I can save the situation by accepting the blame. I apologize, saying there was a misunderstanding on my part. We then walk back to the store, where I ask for the shoes that she had tried on before, those that made her look like a parrot. As I'm watching the lady at the register put those shoes in the box, Ellen asks her if these shoes are okay for walking on cobblestone. She needs to know, it's important, she says. These shoes may not be quite as sturdy as the pair Ellen just returned, the lady replies and adds her personal opinion: "But I think they look a bit more stylish."

Ellen answers with an absultely grim expression on her face: "But I want shoes for walking comfortably on any kind of terrain, especially on those awful pavements in those towns here. I have a bad back and a terrible case of fibromyalgia."

It's highly unlikely that this sales lady knows what fibromyalgia is, let alone how, with people like Ellen, brain biology is connected to physical characteristics. She is a professional, and instead of commenting on Ellen's health problem she says: "Well, then maybe you should take the shoes you returned. They are fine for cobblestone, and you might even be able to hike in them for a good stretch before you might have a problem."

"I can't hike, " Ellen says, loud enough for everyone in the store to hear her. I have two children, I can't just go away and go hiking. Do *you* have children?" The intonation in her question tells me that she thinks this lady is childless and, therefore, has no understanding of the burden you bear with young children.

"No, but I know what you mean."

"No, you can't," she cries. "You don't know."

At this point, the lady, with a name tag saying „Barfuß," shrugs her shoulder. "I am sorry. Is there anything else I can do for you?"

Ellen turns away, so I ask Ms. Barfuß, if she would be so kind to credit my account for the shoes we returned - which she does. We are hardly out of the store, when Ellen demands that I take the shoes back to the store. "But why?" I ask.

"I don't want them, that's why."

Courageously I say: "I think *you* should take them back, if you don't want them."

"No, *you* take them back. *You* paid for them."

"Only because I had my credit card at hand."

"Yeah, you used your card because you wanted to show everybody in the store that you are the one in this family who earns money."

"I don't think anyone in that store cares where the money to pay for your shoes comes from. This is a business, not a social movement organization."

"Don't be asinine. Money carries political power and also symbolic power. *He* earns the money and *she* gets a gift from him every now and then to make her shut up. I saw the look on that woman's face, the look that says I'm your pretty woman. But I'm not, I'm not your *pretty woman*."

In case you don't know, with "pretty woman" she is referring to that film with Julia Roberts. She hates the role this actress plays, the role of the innocent little girl with the unblemished skin and big eyes who wants to be picked up by her daddy to sit on his lap. A woman who thinks she has everything she needs when she struts down the street and walks into a high-class hotel in her knee-high leather boots and newest fashion dress, which she just bought with the credit card that a wealthy and absolutely good-looking man so graciously gave her and told her she should feel free to splurge, so that he would be happy too when they both sit together with his business friends at the dinner table in an expensive restaurant.

Has she ever brought this up with you? Has she ever told you how morally superior she feels over the other women in her social circle because she is the only one who has a carefully thought-out opinion about the role Julia Roberts plays in that film? I have colleagues who tell me that they don't know any woman who is not in love with that film. And those women who don't love this film love Julia Roberts. Even unshakeable feminists love her. One colleague says about his radical feminist girlfriend that, statistically speaking, chances are that eventually she will love Julia Roberts too. Well, I don't agree with him when he says that women think that if you can get through life batting your eye lashes, it beats the hell out of carrying your own shopping bags. And if there is such a rule, Ellen is an exception to it. She has never used flirtatiousness as a strategy, at least not with me. Batting eyelashes is out of the question for her, and if she ever showed helplessness, it was definitely not feigned. She *is* helpless, and probably has always been.

Without waiting for my response to her assertion that people in that store thought of her as "my pretty woman," she orders me to go back to the store with her. I'm not sure what she's up to now. Return the shoes, get a second pair of shoes, explain to the sales lady that she is not *any*body's "pretty woman"? Once in the store, she goes directly to the woman at the cash register, puts her own credit card on the counter, and demands that the purchase be redirected from my account to hers. Of course, this woman has no idea why Ellen is making this request, so it's up to me to provide an explanation. There is no problem with the account, I say. It's just that my wife wants to try out her new credit card.

Should I have told her the truth, Doctor? Ellen wouldn't have understood what I could have said, if I had spoken in a strong Bavarian dialect. I could have said, I am very sorry, Ms. Barfuß, but my wife is not feeling well today, or, more to the truth, she doesn't mean to hassle *you*, she's trying to get at *me*. Would it have harmed anybody if I had been *completely* honest? Ms. Barfuß, my wife is miserable, annoyed, and confused. She has a mind of her own, a mind which hasn't been working all that well, for years. You should know that she has gone through a lot. She had electric shocks run through her brain and she has tried out all kinds of psycho drugs to cure depression, hysteric fits, panic attacks, irritable bowel syndrome, yeast syndrome, chronic fatigue syndrome, and a whole slew of other syndromes you probably never heard of. What she has gone through you wouldn't wish for your worst enemy. So please excuse her and please be so kind and do the billing once more, this time using *her* credit card. Please do me that favor, I beg you, or I'm dead.

So this is how I managed the end of act II. I didn't say any of this to this woman, no surprise there. My ultimate goal was to get through the next few days in one piece, and for this it was irrelevant who paid for those shoes. Ms. Barfuß refused to redo the billing, which I explained to Ellen by referring to administrative difficulties that could not be resolved until the following week. She wasn't happy with this explanation at all. I should have tried much harder making her case, she said, I should have told "this twit" that whatever administrative problem her store might have was nothing compared to what she had to contend with.

The result of all this going back and forth was that Ellen kept the shoes and that we skipped a visit to Calw and, instead, drove straight to my mother's house. I explained to Ellen my decision to go to Freising rightaway by pointing out that it was getting too late to return to the Black Forest, because we would be driving through Freudenstadt a fourth or a fifth time, which she surely would have a problem with, given her aversion against this city, with the church being tucked away in the corner, on top of getting stuck in rush-hour traffic at this time of the day. Ellen didn't protest. I think she was much too exhausted at this point to resist.

Before we left Altensteig, I stopped at a phone booth to call my mother to let her know that we would be arriving at her house a day earlier than planned. She didn't say that our early arrival was or was not okay with her, but I heard her heavy breathing, which I interpreted as a sign that she was not looking forward to seeing us so soon.

The Failed Conversion

We arrived in Freising just before ten o'clock in the evening, too late for Ellen and my mother to get into a fight, although the few words they exchanged made it clear to me that they both had problems holding back what they would like to say to each other. My mother waited until Ellen disappeared in the bathroom to get ready for bed and then asked me if there was something wrong with her. "Your wife hasn't said much. Is something the matter?" I had told her some time ago that Ellen was on the way to getting better. I had said this to keep my mother from repeating what she had been saying to me for years, that I shouldn't have married "this woman." Now I said that there was nothing wrong with Ellen other than that she was struggling with the most awful jetlag and with fatigue from driving around the Black Forest for the last two days. To confirm the reason for Ellen's bad mood, I said that I was terribly exhausted too.

Later, in bed, Ellen asked me if there was something wrong with my mother, she had hardly spoken to her. She had expected a more enthusiastic welcome from her, she said. After all, they had not seen each other for several years. The excuse I invented for my mother's silence was that she was still in mourning over the death of my father. The evenings were usually the most difficult time of day for her, I said. She'd be more talkative in the morning.

Talkative she was, yes, but not in a way you would call welcoming, or at least diplomatically polite. The atmosphere at the breakfast table was extremely tense. The confrontation started with my mother asking Ellen how she liked the Black Forest, and Ellen shooting back: "Not much. Or how would *you* like driving behind diesel trucks all the time?" My mother had wanted to hear something else, something like, "Oh, it's even nicer there than I thought," but of course she should have known better. The two of them had not been on good terms from the very beginning of their relationship, starting with an episode which I had never told Ellen about.

I remember that episode clearly. A few months after I had met Ellen I had shown my mother a photograph of her. Naïve as I was at that time I thought she would be happy to know that I was involved with a woman whom I considered pretty, intelligent, and interesting in so many different ways. I expected her to say something positive, something encouraging and endearing, and to show her curiosity by asking me where I had met her. But she reacted in the most hateful way you can imagine. I remember her looking at this photograph with utmost contempt, as if I was showing her a report card with F's on it. And she made a nasty comment on her eyes. Bulging eyes, she said, they look like they are popping out of their socket, and her nose is weird and pointy. She might as well have said, "Look, you got yourself a witch!"

I should have known better. Forget tactfulness, my mother has never been particularly kind to any of the women I had introduced to her. Depending on how they presented themselves and articulated their interests, she called them "radical," "flimsy," "women's libber," or just "strange," meaning they weren't someone she would accept as a daughter-in-law. But her rejection of Ellen, even before she had a chance to meet her in person, was of an entirely new quality. I had not expected this kind of nasty reaction when I handed her the photograph. She held it between her fingers, as if she thought she might catch gonorrhea from it.

I didn't have the courage to stand up to her and tell her that I was going on thirty and perfectly capable of deciding whom I wanted to live with. I felt like a six-year-old who climbs on his mother's lap when he has done something wrong. She spent a lot of energy commenting on Ellen's "balloon eyes," as she called them, saying there is something wrong with her. Those were her words, *something wrong*. I should stay away from her, she's trouble, she said with nothing but contempt in her voice.

The concept she bets on, when she's afraid she won't get her way, is guilt. Now *that* should interest you. You see, she's the kind of mother who makes sure you never forget who gave birth to you and who says to you when you are a little child: Who does Mommy love more than anyone else in the world? How can you ignore that?! Now that I am much older she gives me "advice" and she lets me know that the advice comes from a mother who is always concerned about her son's health, his safety, his emotional well-being, in fact, his entire future. "Why can't I give you advice, why don't you *ever* listen to me? I am your mother, I only say this for your own good. Why do you reject *everything* I am saying?" Those are the typical phrases she throws at me when I have the gall to do my own thing. I should concentrate on my studies, instead of getting involved with a woman, she said. My staying with Ellen would be a serious mistake. I shouldn't let someone like her ruin my future.

And as if Ellen's balloon eyes weren't enough to get me to give her up, she also brought up her last name. Schleppy is a silly name, she said, it's a laugh. Who in the world is called Schleppy, except a puppy dog maybe? It sounds like a name you give to someone not quite right in his head. Those were her words, Doctor, the words of a mother who cares about my future. I told her that this name comes from someone who had immigrated from Switzerland and changed his name from something like Schleppi or Schläppi to Schleppy. If you can believe this, for a moment I felt like a grown-up. I mounted a sarcastic protest, saying that the solution to the name problem lied in me marrying her. Instead of Ellen Schleppy she would be called Ellen Köhnlechner.

But now my mother really tore into me. She called me a fool. She had not given up so much of her life so that I would turn into a fool. The whole neighborhood would laugh at *her* if I married "this woman." I hadn't studied all these years at an expensive and excellent university to end up with *her*. "This gypsy" would wreck my life, she said. She'd latch on to me and take advantage of me, of my dependability, my talents, and my money. I told her that Ellen would be earning her own money. With her degree in psychology she might even do better than me. I actually believed what I said, given what I had read about psychologists finding well-paid employment in a wide range of fields. Psychologists are more in demand than sociologists, I told her, and also that Ellen planned to study for a second degree. A double degree in psychology and something else would open up career opportunities in a wide variety of fields.

A reasonable argument, I thought at that time, but to my mother this was utter nonsense. She said I was stupid assuming that Ellen would go back to university once she was married to me. She called me naïve and childish, and told me about the women in her neighborhood, none of whom were working outside the home because they were married to men who earned well. Mrs. Bergmüller had a cleaning lady come to her house twice a week because she considered herself too good for holding a broom, and Mrs. Klier went horseback riding every second afternoon, so she could show everyone what exquisite taste she has. And what could Ellen achieve with her undergraduate degree, compared to what I could do with my doctorate, she asked, a woman who proudly took care of her household all by herself and wouldn't dream of sitting on a horse. When she was finished with her tirade, she took one more look at Ellen's photo, holding it in her hand as if she inspected the picture of a working-class prostitute I was going to live with.

I'm pretty sure that one reason for being so rough on Ellen - at this stage it was just her picture - is the disappointment I caused her when I went to the States at the age of twenty to be with a young woman I had fallen in love with and to attend university in her country. My going away had upset my parents' family planning in a most fundamental way. They had expected that I would study at a university near them and would come home every weekend to get some rest from my studies, while my mother would happily feed me my favorite dishes, do my laundry, and mend my socks. My going overseas was like stabbing a knife into her belly, and each time I changed to another university in the States to continue my studies there, rather than coming home, ripped that gaping wound open again. So my announcement before completing my doctorate studies that I would not return home, but would live with an American woman, who, I said, was "pretty, intelligent, and interesting," and showing my mother a photograph of her to prove it, meant to her that I would never come back into her fold.

I had never told Ellen about this episode with my mother because I didn't want to influence her way of building a relationship with her. I also felt ashamed having a mother who wouldn't even think of giving her adult son's girlfriend a chance. Of course, I did not heed her warning about continuing my involvement with Ellen, but I should have made more of an effort to discuss with her how she came to the conclusion that Ellen wasn't right for me. Even if her reasoning was contaminated by fears that had more to do with herself than with me, I might have learned *something* of use to me. To this day I wonder how it could be that my mother, who I never thought of as a person with much social intelligence, would be so "wise" to recognize in a photograph of Ellen something that *I* did not discover until I had been married to her for five years.

Given everything she had said about Ellen in the past, why would I be surprised now that our visit with her would be anything but pleasant? I must have been out of my mind to have expected that things between my mother and Ellen had changed for the better. My mother was angry about having Ellen in her house for the next three days, and Ellen was upset having to sit at the table of a woman she had looked at with disdain for the last ten years and believing that I had always given preference to my mother's wishes over hers. She was far too resentful to be able to carry on a meaningful conversation with my mother.

After breakfast, Ellen withdrew into our room, where she stayed until lunchtime. The few times I went upstairs to check on her I saw her either flipping through a magazine she had picked up on our flight, rummaging through her suitcase, or standing at the window and staring out into the garden, where my mother was tending to her flowers. I had the distinct feeling that she was busying herself so as not to have to confront Ellen. She was outside in the garden by herself moping, and Ellen was in our room by herself ruminating. From what Ellen said to my mother later that day and the following day you'd think she was confused over whether she should terminate or renew her relationship with her. At lunchtime she talked as if she wanted to kick her out of her life once and for all, and a mere twenty-four hours later she wanted nothing more than to have her in the center of her social circle.

On that first day my mother had made rice pudding for lunch, prepared the way she had done it as long as I can remember. It was delicious, as always, but for Ellen it wasn't good enough, or rather, rice pudding was completely out of the question. It wasn't something to be served as a full meal, she said. In America rice pudding was considered a dessert, not a main dish. If my mother wanted rice pudding to be a sweet dish, which is what the word "pudding" implied – although the German term for it doesn't have the word "pudding" in it and doesn't imply sweetness –, she should put fresh fruit in it, preferably apples or pears, rather than raisins, and definitely not processed raisins. She should heed Ellen's nutritional expertise and use ingredients fresh from the garden. And equally important, my mother should cook only with whole-grain rice. Ellen explained in detail – I translated diligently because she insisted that my mother learn something, for her own good, she said – the nutritional value of whole-grain rice compared to that of processed rice. Rice pudding made with whole-grain rice isn't only healthier, it also tastes much better. She could also mix vegetables in with the rice, if she wanted to be really original, to which my mother replied that it was then no longer rice pudding, but "some sort of vegetable mush."

My mother was terribly offended by Ellen's intervention, although she didn't *say* that she was hurt. I know how to read the look on her face when she dishes out her rice pudding and wonders if she should throw a spoonful of white rice into Ellen's face. How dare you criticize my cooking, the look says. Your whole-grain rice pudding, this vegetable mishmash, your fresh-fruit garbage, whole-meal this, whole-meal that, all of that is just shit. What audacity you have to tell me my rice pudding is too sweet for your hypersensitive tummy of yours, which, by the way, isn't all that small. If you don't like my rice pudding, don't eat so much of it. *That* would be good for your health – and for your waistline too!

After lunch, when we were upstairs in our room, Ellen told me how terribly insulted she feels by what my mother had said to her. "But she didn't say anything," I pointed out.

"But it's so obvious what she was *thinking*. If she had any interest in learning from me, she would have discussed with me what I said about wholesome cooking. Instead, I ate that awfully sweet stuff."

"Why did you, if you think it's not healthy?"

"Because I am polite. I have manners, she doesn't. She knows that I only eat whole-meal, she has known this for years, it's not the first time that I am in her house. It's the same with her Apfelstrudel and those steamed yeast dumplings she makes. It's all much too sweet. And it's a dessert, not a main dish. Everyone knows this, you know it too, but you don't defend me, you don't say anything to her."

I didn't say anything to my mother because it's just too ridiculous to comment on this silly quarrelling about dumplings. Two grown women fighting over the appropriateness of rice pudding as a main meal is beyond me. When I answered Ellen that me saying something to my mother would make things worse, because my mother "feels a bit unsure" in her presence, she yelled at me. "Why should she be unsure? She has known me now for almost fifteen years. I have been nice to her from the beginning, but after all these years she is still adamantly set against me. She has never made any effort to really talk to me, and she has never shown any interest in any of the things I am good at. There is so much I could teach her, if she would only let me. But she prefers to look the other way, because if she would listen to me, she would have to admit that I am right. God knows how hard I tried with her. I don't understand why she is so negative towards me. I am still young, I look good, and I am bright. I don't deserve the way she treats me."

To escape my mother for a few hours, for Ellen's sake and for mine, I suggested that we go into town for the afternoon and do some window shopping. She wasn't exactly thrilled walking around town in the hot sun, but when she saw the two steeples of the cathedral up on the hill, she knew where she wanted to be. A few minutes later we were inside the cathedral.

I sat down in the last row, watching her as she wandered around the cathedral, looking at the paintings over the arches and on the ceiling, the pulpit, and the organ over the entrance, although I had the distinct impression that she wasn't interested in anything she saw. After a good fifteen minutes of walking around, she knelt down in front of the altar and then took a seat on a bench close to the pulpit. I think she spent well over an hour sitting there, before she stood up, looked at the altar for a long time, and then, walking past me absolutely stonefaced, she went outside.

I caught up with her outside, where I found her sitting in a comatose state on the steps of a neighboring building. I sat down next to her, waiting for her to say something. After a few minutes she said, without looking at me, that I was not "normal," just like my mother and most of the doctors she had consulted these last few years. No one had taken her seriously, she said. They had not properly "diagnosed" her needs, just like I "never paid attention" to her needs.

When I asked her what her needs were that I supposedly never paid attention to, she replied: "Fifteen years and you still don't know!" She said she had just spoken with God, and He had told her to let go of me. But she couldn't, because she was married to me and she was taking the sacrament of marriage seriously. She told Him this - I suppose this means she had an argument with God - and eventually He said that she should give it another try. It would help her get well, and then she could get on with her life. "Don't you want to have a wife who is well?" she asked.

Forgive me if I sound a bit cynical now. She can't have a reasonable conversation with my mother, not even for five minutes, but she can converse with God for an hour and then tell me what big difference a frank talk with God can make. "Yes," I say, "get well, I'm all for it."

The truth is, I had already reached the point where I no longer expected that she would ever get well. It was her behavior at that road fork yesterday which convinced me that there was nothing more I could do for her - or that I *wanted* to do for her. She'll be stuck in her misery forever, I'm saying to myself, as I watch her stare at the cobblestone walkway across the yard. Is she afraid the cobblestone will ruin her feet when we go back into town? With my luck she'll ask me to carry her home, so I repeat what I had said: "Get well, you know what to do."

And this is her answer: "Yes, and if you read my literature, you would know what *you* have to do."

"What literature?" Of course I know what literature she means. It's in that big box she brought to your office for you to keep. You had asked for it, remember? You wanted her to get her mind off this stuff. But it didn't work. Spending a few days not reading about vitamin supplements or Bible reinterpretations, that's out of the question. Not even two weeks later she picked up her box again.

She says: "Don't do this to me. You know exactly what literature I mean."

"The literature on bowel cleansing or the books on the yeast syndrome?" I remind her that her homemade therapy of nothing but cooked vegetables had made her even sicker. They had put her in the hospital for weeks, and it took a lot of psychiatric intervention to get her on her feet again. She had wanted to put our children on that crazy diet too. If I hadn't stopped her, they would have ended up in the hospital too.

"No, I'm talking about my books on near-death experiences. It really wouldn't hurt you to read this. You always say you want new insights."

Insights? I call it mumbo jumbo! She argued that the fact that so many people who "came back" after having died reported the same visions, hovering above their own body, traveling through a tunnel towards a bright light at the other end, and then deciding to return to their ordinary life, that all this was proof of life after death. I said that these reported experiences were chemical reactions in the brain of people under serious stress, that pleasant emotions were the result of the brain releasing endorphins, that stimulating the temporal lobes can induce floating sensations and feelings of religious significance, and that when cells in the visual system fire randomly, they produce the effect of seeing a bright light in the middle of that system. In my opinion, all these biological reactions are the result of an evolutionary development to help humans deal with stress, so even mumbo jumbo can be of some value. Let her believe what she wants, as long as she leaves me alone with this.

It is quite possible that in twenty years she will deny what she said about near-death experiences, life after death, alien kidnapping, and this other crazy stuff she believes in. But I kept a diary of most everything, and when my children are old enough and have gained sufficient distance from that part of their history, and they are in a position where they can apply their intelligence without their mother breathing down their neck, I will show them my diary, together with documents I collected, including police affidavits and e-mails from colleagues, and then we will have a frank discussion about their mother.

Now, Ellen has just spent an hour conversing with God who, she says, recommended that I read that literature so that I may discover the truth too. Doctor, I know the truth. The truth is that her brain is gone, isn't that so? The kind of brain you need to know that it *is* possible to sleep in a bed with a gap between mattresses. She talks about a bright light at the other end of a tunnel and happy angel faces greeting her there, and I would really like to say to her: Ellen, what are you waiting for? Go and find that tunnel. But I don't say this, because I feel so ashamed just thinking how wonderful it would be if she did end up in some tunnel and never came back. She sits there and wants me to discuss out-of-body events, and I just want to get up and run around this cathedral a few times.

During dinner my mother asks me where we had been all afternoon, which of the tourist sites in town we had visited. What should I say? If I told her that Ellen had spent most of the afternoon in the cathedral, not for the purpose of admiring the rococo decorations and restored frescoes, but to get spiritual insight into what she could do to reform me, what would my poor mother say to me, the son who didn't listen to her warnings about Ellen? If I told her that Ellen wanted to talk to me about out-of-body stuff, I might as well tell her about the exorcism she had a priest perform in our house a few months ago. Look what I have to put up with, I could say. Even if I had two doctorates I couldn't do anything about this sort of thing.

Do you know that story? No? Well, imagine this scene. I come home from the office in the early afternoon, and when I go into my bedroom to change my clothes, I find Ellen and a couple strangers standing next to my bed, an elderly man dressed in a black suit and a young woman with hair down to the waist. Ellen had asked them to perform an exorcism of all rooms in our house, they say. They call it "the full package deal" and smile tellingly. Maybe they think the house is full of evil spirits. The two kids' rooms they had already "done," and now they are about to start in the bedroom. I could throw them out right then and there, but I am polite. I don't want make a scene, meaning I don't want to embarrass Ellen.

She tells me that she had paid "this nice gentleman and his young lady" in advance the "measly sum of one hundred and fifty dollars." One hundred and fifty dollars is not a big deal, I say to myself, as I watch the exorcist sweep with both hands across the mattress – a queensize mattress with no gap –, first from the left, then backwards again, and then from the top down, while mumbling something to his assistant, who is reading from a book something I don't understand, something about mysteries of incarnation, flames of hell, and the carnal presence of the forbidden. Maybe I rolled my eyes or let out a loud sigh, because Ellen says to me, in a very hostile tone of voice: "You don't understand, because you don't have faith." Then she gives the exorcist instructions for what to do next. He should continue with the upstairs bathroom, as this is the room, apart from the bedroom, where she has been feeling most uncomfortable lately. Then he should go downstairs and "do" the kitchen, and then the living-room. The basement he could safely ignore.

I am *extremely* polite, I must say. I ask no questions and I don't do anything that would disturb the holy ceremony. The only point where I say something is when, on the way from the kitchen to the living-room, I announce that they could skip the toilet. No chance of evil spirits being there. I say this jokingly because I want to loosen up the atmosphere, which is very tense.

As the two of them are getting ready to leave, I ask them if they had picked up anything unusual, if they had heard any unfamiliar noises, like a rumbling, knocking, or hissing, if they had noticed coloration in the walls, or if there are any strange smells they had come across. To make my questions appear legitimate I tell them that I am a professor at the university, that I look at things which cannot be observed directly, like opinions and sentiments, very critically, scientifically that is. They should excuse my asking these questions, because critical analysis is at the core of my training. It's what keeps me going.

The boss in this team looks at Ellen, as if to ask her for support, but then he comes up with his own response. He says what he is doing is outside the "regular sciences," but it is just as important for maintaining a healthy human spirit as, say, the work of pharmacists. He had not noticed anything that would indicate the presence of evil forces in our house, but I should see his work as a prophylactic measure. I smile and reply that at a price of one hundred and fifty dollars taking prophylactic measures is not "out of this world." He looks at Ellen again, who is now just a few inches away from reprimanding me for being sarcastic. One should not take this too lightly, he says. Evil forces can wreak havoc with the human soul. His "procedures" are designed to take care of this before things get out of hand.

As a last act before leaving he and his assistant stop in the hallway for a minute to give the matter one last look and to reassure Ellen – me they ignore at this point – that things are well under control now. He advises her to look at the exorcism ritual as a holy act and explains this by reading three short passages from the Bible, while his assistant dips her fingers into a small urn the size of a pickle jar and sprinkles some liquid first onto the floor and then onto the wall on both sides. So that is that, mission completed.

I hadn't told anybody about this except one of my colleagues, who thought it was funny and so unlike me, a die-hard pragmatist and unshakable atheist, to let an exorcist step into my bedroom. Now I'm thinking about telling my mother that Ellen had an exorcist come to our house in search of those nasty forces that had driven her crazy. My mother would't say anything in front of Ellen, I'm sure, but later, when we are alone, she'd tear into me. I had allowed my "gypsy wife" to have someone perform a ritual that belongs to the Middle Ages, she'd say. So no, I won't tell her, and I also won't tell her that Ellen spent half the afternoon in church praying. I'm in absolutely no mood to defend Ellen's praying, so what I say to my mother is that we ran into an old friend of mine and then sat in a cafe with him, chatting for a couple of hours.

What a mistake! Ellen grabs my mother's wrist and says: "Bernd is lying, your son is lying. There was no friend at all. He doesn't want to tell you where we were. We were in the cathedral where I spoke with

God. Your son is lying. He does this often, you know. Did you know that he once told me that he had an uncle who lived in Uruguay after the war, where he owned a cocoa plantation? I learned in college that many Germans who emigrated to South America were Nazis. These were people who wanted to escape prosecution. So I believed him until he said that it was a joke. But Gerda, you don't joke about such matters. What if we had a Nazi in our family? Why would he come up with a lie like this and then say it's just a joke? And there are also other things that your son thinks are a joke, running around the garden naked for example."

If you can believe this, my ultrahumanitarian wife thinks it's her duty to tell my mother about my being outside without any clothes on. And she is lying! Why? Did God tell her to come up with a cockamamie story like that? *I did not run around the garden.* I stood on our terrace, in the middle of the summer, when it was thirty-five degrees in the shade. Big deal! Other people spend a whole summer in a nudist park. I know someone who goes skinny dipping on a public beach in broad daylight. And there are people who do nudist camping, nudist hiking, nudist mountain climbing, nudist horseback riding, and God knows what else, whereas I merely stood on our own terrace for maybe a minute or two, no longer than it takes to put on your socks and shoes. My mother is shocked by what Ellen is telling her. She shakes her head irritably, while Ellen is beaming with joy, having gotten my mother to question my sanity. I don't say anything. Why? Because it's too stupid to turn this into a topic for discussion.

But Doctor, this is only the beginning. Because she now has my mother's full attention, she dumps on her all kinds of stuff about me that she thinks needs to be corrected. She speaks with absolute clarity of purpose about the son who should be in reform school, not necessarily to be punished for his vile conduct – though sitting in a dark confessional for an hour wouldn't be so bad –, but to be shown a path for improvement. And these are the main items on her list of complaints. She wants to have a third child and says that this would be "good" for me, but I refuse to give her what "is only natural." I am also not sleeping with her as often as what "the whole world considers normal." And I refuse to go to church with her, I don't support her in something that is written in the constitution. For her to get the full benefit out of Mass and to feel the spirit when listening to a sermon, she needs to have her husband kneeling next to her. By not being with her in church I am depriving her of all this. How exactly this deprivation comes about, what psychological mechanisms are at work, she doesn't say.

Now, I could of course set the record straight. I wouldn't be lying at all if I told my mother that her hypermoralist, pious daughter-in-law had the habit, on a hot summer day and under God's watchful eyes, of sitting half or fully naked on our balcony at home. What would my mother say to *that*? And what if I told her that Ellen had let Marcus suck on her breast from time to time when he was six or seven years old. I could also declare that I never kept Ellen from going to church or from studying the Bible forwards, backwards, sideways, or in any direction she pleased. And since Ellen mentioned constitutional rights, I could announce that I have rights too, that it is *my* constitutional right *not* to accompany her to church. I have the right to stay home. And this thing about not being able to pray, that's rubbish. Ellen has been praying day and night, quietly in her head and publicly in church, and today she was in the cathedral for over an hour praying, without me interfering in any way.

I *could* say all this to my mother, and at this point I could also give her my list of the not exactly conventional activities Ellen has been engaged in for the last six or seven years, all of which I supported more or less actively, or endured in a muted sort of way, and which cost me - my mother was right, she never earned a cent with her college degree - quite a bit of money. These are, in no particular order: hormone therapy, aroma therapy, vitamin B complex therapy, marital therapy, talk therapy, drug therapy, acupuncture, hypnosis, far-eastern meditation, chiropractic interventions like Rolfing and Gonstead adjustment, and a few other things I can't remember, or she never told me about. There is also her conviction that she has been suffering from the yeast syndrome, from fibromyalgia, and from critters crawling under her scalp, all things requiring serious attention.

I had never told my mother any of this, to spare Ellen the ridicule she'd draw from her, but also because I didn't want to hear my mother remind me that she had told me to keep my fingers off her. My mother saying that I never listen to her motherly advice, and Ellen saying that I never listen to her wifely needs is a deadly combination as far as the image that I have of myself is concerned. These two needy women are now facing each other at the dinner table and I am sitting between them, unable to say more than a few words. Oh, I wish I had the guts to grab them both by the arm and yell at them: "Just stop it, both of you!"

There is no guarantee that telling my mother about Ellen's psychological problems would correct in her head the picture Ellen is painting of me. To my mother I might sound defensive, and Ellen would see my protest as an opportunity to cut into me even more. She'd invent stories of a whole new caliber, I'm sure. You know how theatrical she is when she begins an argument with her favorite words, "But you don't understand," and then she works on you so you do understand. Why wouldn't I understand? Fifteen years of listening to my hypermoralist companion, of course I understand. *She* is the one who doesn't understand, least of all herself.

So when she says to my mother, "But you don't understand," I know what's coming. And when she says, "When I was in church today and spoke with God, He told me to talk to you, Gerda, what *you* can do to help your son become a normal person," I finish my tea and announce that I am going to bed. You don't need me in your audience to carry on your show that you so fondly call "Bad Husband, Bad Son."

Now here is the big decision, the decision that had lingered in my head all evening. I now knew what I had to do. When I left the table I decided that I would send Ellen home the next day, because, Doctor, as far as I am concerned, this so-called vacation was over. And let me tell you, making this decision had a wonderfully liberating effect on me. No more whining, no more yelling, and no more ordering me around. I felt de-Ellenized even before I told her my decision. When I went to bed I didn't care what these two women downstairs were talking about, and I didn't care how Ellen would react when she wakes up the next morning and hears me say to her: "Look, this is no vacation for you. You obviously don't feel well, you complain about my mother's rice pudding, your feet hurt from walking on cobblestone, and you say that I don't let you drive the car, and when you do drive, you say that I forced you to drive so that you get lost. You want to talk to God about all this, which is fine with me, but I think you can do that at home as well, in English, on your time, and in the church of your liking. Therefore, considering everything you say you want and don't get, I think it's best that you go home today."

That's exactly what I said to her the next morning. To my surprise she didn't protest when I went to a travel agency to rebook her return flight at nearly double the original ticket price. I was lucky to have gotten her a seat on a flight leaving out of Frankfurt in late afternoon. There would be plenty of time to pack her suitcase, have a small lunch, and then drive her to the airport. Once she is checked in at the airport, she will have to manage on her own. It'll be good practice for her, because I won't be around anymore to do those chores for her. After landing in Toronto, she will drive our car, which we had parked near the airport, to her parents' home in upstate New York and then she will stay with them and our children until my return a week and a half later.

She hardly spoke to me that morning, and at lunchtime she was mostly quiet too. It was only when my mother said something about Ellen probably looking forward to seeing our children, that she let off steam, demonstrating her theatrical talent. You'd think she was a regimental sergeant who had picked up a few ideas about confession and conversion while touring the Vatican. I don't remember everything she said in that sanctimonious presentation, but some of what she said is still in my head so clearly that I can quote her now.

She accosted my mother for having raised a son with a personality disorder of the kind that one typically develops early in childhood. She said she was able to categorize my problem as a borderline personality disorder because she had studied psychology in college. One of the main lessons she had learned is that you can tell the cause of something by looking at symptoms. My refusal to close the top button of my shirt at our wedding ceremony is one such symptom of my personality disorder, another one is my insisting to not get married in a church. She said she had let this go at the time because she didn't want to be the nagging wife from the beginning. Aren't I lucky?!

A serious problem occurs, she said, citing some basic concept from Psychology 101, when the child doesn't feel loved as a whole being. "What have you done, Gerda, that your son has developed this kind of existential insecurity, which is so strong that he won't even trust his own wife to help him? I have so many books he could read, but he refuses. He is not normal, Gerda. If he were normal, he would take an active part in my academic interests." She also said that she had tried to get me to seek professional help, but that I refused, claiming that I didn't need help, that I'd rather spend my time working on a paper, as if I needed to write another paper. And when I finally did go see a psychologist – she insisted on coming along –, I talked with him more about her than about myself. Talking more about her than about myself is in itself symptomatic of my personality disorder, she said.

You should have been there, hearing all that nonsense she was unloading on my mother. Is this the result of those hundred plus sessions you have had with her? Five years of analysis, talking cure, anxiety pills, and what have you, and she concludes that I wasn't brought up as a "whole being." Does she think I'm half a being? And which of the two halves is responsible for my nasty borderline personality disorder? The half that my mother ignored, or the other half that she nurtured to become what I am now? She asked my mother what she would say, if her son ran naked through *her* garden, on a Sunday, the day of the Lord, in the middle of the day, when the sun is shining bright and everybody can see me? Mind you, even if I *had* been hopping around our garden, our house is basically in the woods, and there is absolutely no possibility of any of the neighbors getting a glimpse of me.

And get this, now she is telling my mother that I have "behavioral issues" in the groin. I sometimes touch myself in the area between the inner thigh and the testicles, she says, using exact those words, and I do this in front of three-year-old Chrissie. She makes it sound as if I'm putting on a show for the kid. Doctor, I beg you, you must talk to her about this. Tell her that after jogging fifteen miles I'm hot and sweaty when I come home. My underwear is soggy from sweat and my shorts are pungent. I'd feel great, if there weren't this awful itch in the groin. When the skin on the inner thighs rubs together, there is chafing. The skin is irritated, it burns like hell, so I scratch myself. For God's sake, what's wrong with scratching? I don't get it!

"What did you do that your son turned out like this, that he would do such a thing?" she says to my mother who is in a stupor by now. "And he doesn't care that Chrissie sees him." Doctor, as if a three-year-old pays attention to this. There are six-year-olds who sit in the sauna with their parents, and they don't end up with a personality disorder. Saint Ellen of course knows otherwise. "You didn't bring him up right, Gerda. There are so many things you should have done differently. I am saying this not to criticize you, but because I love you."

Oh, I see, the human-rights fanatic now *loves* my mother. Is that why she talks in such loving detail about me running around the garden naked and scraching myself in the groin? Christ Almighty, you'd think I was masturbating in front of city hall. I knew she had a malicious streak, but now she talks to my mother as if I'm a child molester. I was livid. And I hate it when she puts a hand on her heart and speaks in that all-knowing, holier-than-holy tone that she adopts when she thinks she has something very important to say and everybody has to listen. And my mother did listen. You should have seen the look on her face, an amalgam of shock, disgust, and contempt.

Have you ever had someone in your office complaining to their mother-in-law that her son is scratching himself in the crotch after jogging? With Ellen this kind of talking is genetic, it runs in her family. Her mother is also very uninhibited about things that most people keep to themselves. She complains to me about her husband not doing in bed with her what she wants him to do, because his oversized stomach gets in the way. One of Ellen's aunts asked me once, without the lightest trace of shyness, if I couldn't talk to *her* husband about the idea of "going down on her." And the husband of another aunt of hers told me about the adulterous adventures of his wife, insinuating that he was contemplating similar moves with a woman he knew from church. Ellen's sister tells stories – no embarrassment there either – at the dinner table of her balancing coins on the tip of her younger brother's penis, when they played in the bathtub together as children. Doctor, these people don't even bother hiding their problems under the decorum of Christian piety. They talk about family and about forgiveness and love, but first they expose the person guilty of transgression, because how can you forgive someone who doesn't apologize? If you think Ellen's therapy isn't going anywhere, you might want to talk to the whole family. I'm not saying this to be facetious. Don't psychiatrists normally pay attention to the family of patients who, like Ellen, use the word "family" fifty times in each session?

And this is how the prosecution summarized the indictment. "I know we all have strengths and weaknesses. God made us this way. He is always testing us so we can work on improving ourselves. In my family are people who have problems of all kinds, but they know that they can do something about this, because they have God as their guide. In my family we say things like, 'I am sorry' and 'I love you.' *That* is what makes a true family, one that has God in its center." At this point she wanted to take my mother's hand, to show that she "loves" her, I suppose, but my mother pulled her hand away before she could touch it.

And then, after lunch, after I had put her suitcase in the car and we stood outside in the driveway, she staged her unforgettable goodbye performance. She gave my mother a long hug, as if this goodbye were some sort of religious ceremony, and said: "Gerda, I know you are suffering and you are sorry about me not being with Franz." She didn't say what she thought my mother was suffering from, but I know that she was referring to my father's funeral to which she had not been invited. She assumed that my mother felt sorry about having excluded her. The truth is that my mother had never felt sorry about not having invited her to the funeral. "I don't want that little witch to stand at dad's grave," she had said to me.

Ellen had not forgiven my mother for this "monstrous audacity" of hers, as she called it, and now she said to her with that preachy tone in her voice, while giving me a supercilious look that said, Don't think she won't listen to me: "I want you to know, Gerda, that at our table there will always be a place for you, but you must be open to change. You can start by doing something about your son. I know that you can help me with Bernd. You are his mother, and I am begging you to please help me turn him into a normal person. I want him to be a person who can love me, because he sees me as an enrichment in his life, and not just as a wife who is nagging all the time. He must change, for his own sake, and you should change too. You know, it's never too late to change, and …" Here she relaxes the embrace, looks my mother deeply in the eye, and then says: "And Gerda, please learn to pray." She puts her left hand on her heart, and with the other hand she touches my mother's shoulder lightly. "Don't be afraid to pray, God will hear you. He will lead you into our family." God Almighty, this woman sounds like a registered Republican carrying on about God and family. A few words about the nation and she could work as a campaign manager for some Republican running for office.

She doesn't say much during the three hours we are on the Autobahn. She is probably thinking about a couple of grievances she forgot to tell my mother. When she does open her mouth it is to complain that there is no reason to be at the airport more than two hours before departure time. Not true, I am thinking, there is a very good reason to get to the airport early, and that is that I want to be rid of you as soon as possible, because I have felt nauseous all day. Your pretentious attitude with those preposterous claims about me, that sanctimonious gibberish, the conceited tone in your voice, the condescending grimaces you are making when you demand attention to Your Royal Highness, everything about you has irritated me since last night to the point where I just want to vomit. I know this sounds awful, Doctor, but if you had been with us these last three days and had seen what I went through, you'd understand. I'm driving faster than usual because I want this ordeal to be over with. For a while she is yapping so fervently about being at the airport too early that I'm afraid she'll grab the steering wheel any second to drive us off the road. Why didn't I put her on a train?

I am thinking about what my mother said fifteen years ago and what she has repeated in so many words each time Ellen's name came up in a conversation when I visited my parents: "Bernd, she is trouble, don't you see that?" No, I didn't see it, or I didn't *want* to see it. I think my father saw it, but he was much less forward than my mother in letting me know his assessment of her. When he met her the first time, he didn't say very much to me, but I could sense that he wasn't particularly enthused about her. He might have wanted to leave it up to me to discover whatever problems she had, and he trusted my ability to take the necessary steps. And a few years later, after she showed the first signs of what he called the "dysfunctionality of a blind woman on crutches," he suggested, very gently, that I could turn to him if I needed his help in dealing with my predicament.

With "predicament" he meant my getting stuck with a "woman on crutches." But my real predicament was that I refused to accept the idea that I was in a predicament. I was in a state of hubris, you see. I was absolutely convinced that I had wisdom, that from the beginning I had the kind of insights about Ellen one can only have if one is *married* to her. When I met her I thought that, if there ever came a time when she is not well, she should be able to count on me, I would rescue her. And years later it was the pride of a man who had studied in a foreign country, in a foreign language, at major universities, and who had held lectureships and professorships at reputable universities, which kept me from realizing that I could *not* rescue her. I had gone overseas to prove to myself that I could stand on my own two feet. And I had succeeded, obtaining a tenured professorship at a major university. With these accomplishments how could I possibly confess to my father that I had married someone who needed psychiatric care, and that there was no one to blame other than myself for having hooked up with a mental case? And I would have had to make this confession even before it was clear that she wasn't simply neurotic, but clinically depressed, and that she suffered not just from one, but from a variety of affective disorders.

If my father had known her mental condition, I am sure he would have spoken out. And he would have supported me in caring for my children, I am sure of this too. With Ellen's condition not improving, I had raised Marcus and Chrissi under extremely difficult circumstances, and I had managed to keep them unaware of their mother's illness, which was quite a feat. I saw this as evidence of my maturity as a father and of my intelligence as a manager of limited resources. And holding out with Ellen for so long I saw as proof of my strength as a person. The absolute misery I felt living under her thumb, all those frightful moments every time she went haywire with a panic attack about some new illness she thought she had contracted, or will contract any time soon, and all that time I spent driving her from one doctor to the next and sitting with her in some doctor's office, all that was the price

I paid - willingly, that is - for the blindness I suffered from when I met her first. So much for the intelligence of a man with a Ph.D. from an ivy-league university, a man who reads Kafka and Camus on the side - and still doesn't get it!

Have I finally reached the point where I can truly say I'm intelligent? We'll see. I will face serious challenges, getting away from Ellen in one piece, taking care of our children who will soon enter puberty and for that reason alone will require all the guidance I can give them, and doing all this while holding on to my job, the kind of job that has broken the neck of so many of my colleagues.

As I am approaching Frankfurt airport, I am asking myself whether I should drop her off outside the terminal building or go inside with her and accompany her to the check-in counter. If I drop her off outside, I could just stop the car for a minute and, without turning off the engine, I could pull her out of the car, drop her suitcase on the sidewalk, and then drive away, back to my mother where I would then face denunciations from *her*: "What she is saying about you, this thing about running around the garden in the ..., and also this other thing, is this true?"

Of course, she would never use the words Ellen used. She would have her own sure way of letting me know what was right and what was not. And then she'd beat me up again for having married "this gypsy" and she'd remind me of everything she and my father had done for me and, vicariously, for Ellen too, the large monetary gifts they had given us every now and then and, most prominently, the property they had paid for on which we built our house. She'd tell me how generous she had been towards Ellen, in contrast to what we had gotten from Ellen's parents over fifteen years: a refrigerator and a few dishes. "I want my money back," she'll say to me. And she'll repeat what she had been saying about Ellen all these years, picking words from her library of terms she used to describe Ellen's character: insane, wicked, impossible, looney, parasite, and so on. My mother may be shy in the use of direct language, but when it comes to characterizing Ellen she has developed a sizeable vocabulary of quite colorful terms, some of which I wouldn't know how to translate into English without losing the meaning she wants to get across.

As we enter the airport premises I decide to park the car in an underground garage near the terminal she will be leaving from and then to go inside the terminal with her. I will go with her to the check-in counter because I want to be absolutely certain that she gets checked in without delay and that she will be on that plane when I leave the airport. I want her out of my life, at least for the next few days, so that I can concentrate on my research work, and then I'll see how to handle the rest when I'm back in the States.

Our last conversation in the departure lounge outside the security area is brief. We talk about what she will need to do to get to our car in Toronto, and I tell her that I will call her parents as soon as I'm back at my mother's place tonight to let them know that their daughter will be coming to their house a few days earlier and that I will stay in Germany for another week and a half, as originally planned.

It seems she is at the brink of tears. Have I overdone it in cruelty, jumping on her my decision to send her home, and now leaving her in the terminal by herself? She doesn't say anything other than "Well, so that's it," and as I then walk towards the exit I am thinking for a second about going back to say one last word of goodbye to her, because, if you can believe this, I feel sorry for her. But only for a moment, thank God, because when I turn around, expecting her to stand there looking lost and dejected, I see undisguised hatred in her eyes. There is her instinct for moral overkill again, except now it's not in what she says, but in the way she looks at me. It is the trigger-happy look of a Samurai warrier, a look that says, I'll kill you if you come near me. At this moment she looks the very opposite of a woman who not only makes a fuss about her self-appointed beauty, but also has no qualms about showing the world that she has the right to make a fuss because she *is* beautiful. She sits there, throwing hateful looks at me, while clutching her carry-on bag, as if it were a life preserver. She looks godawful, just pathetic. On my way out of the terminal I make a detour to look at the departure board, because I want to be sure that her flight isn't cancelled and that there is no delay.

Home Again

Yes, I am angry, I'm furious. I only need to hear her name, and it all comes up, the absurdity of it all. When we spoke yesterday and I gave you my account of what happened on this trip, it felt a bit like submitting my report to the academy, you know, Kafka's little story. I didn't report to you as if you were one of those highly esteemed gentlemen of the academy, but there are certain similarities between Kafkas intention with his story and what I told you. During this so-called vacation with Ellen I often felt like Kafka's ape in the way I subjected myself to her yoke. On the other hand, and that's the good part, what happened on this outing was enough to bring me to my senses. Unlike Kafka's ape, who needed five years to learn what it requires to be human, it took me only two days, if you think of this episode at that road fork as a seminal moment, to realize that to be human again I need to disengage from her entirely. Two days, I'd call this progress, when you compare this to my six years of living the life of a full-time idiot.

I want to add a few things to what I said yesterday, but mostly I want to tell you what I'm planning to do by way of reconstituting my life. It will take time, and distance will be vital in my convalescence. I don't want to be in a position where I might get reinfected by her neediness, so I want to be absolutely clear of her. My last few years were devoted to her illness, and I was foolish enough to think that I could be part of the solution, just as only a fool would think that taking a fool with me to Germany would cure her. Absurd!

I am a scientist, so I am allergic to absurdity. In my research I prefer to work with variables I can control, in settings in which I can make observations objectively. If I have variables whose validity and reliability cannot be established, and if I operate in a setting that affects me personally, I get extremely nervous. In your field you are at risk of countertransference, so you should appreciate what I'm saying about personal feelings. What happened on that trip with Ellen really has nothing to do with science. Irrational decision-making, unfocused anger, and underlying hostility ruled everything that she said and did, and my response to this wasn't always what I would call controlled. It was all emotion and bad psychology with all its faulty inferences and misguided perceptions that I was struggling with.

You said she should look at this trip as an opportunity to relax and to leave her bad thoughts at home. You said she might meet new people. What new people? The waitress in the hotel restaurant, who didn't bring her the poached eggs she wanted, or the man with his smelly dog? You mean those new people?

Well yes, she met them, but she didn't really talk with them. If she spoke with anyone more than a few sentences, it was my mother, but she talked *to* her, not *with* her, and it was the old quarrel that she was so happy living out again. Maybe she didn't have Betty Friedan on her reading list in college. Why else would she cling to that neo-Freudian myth that everybody's ills should be blamed on their mother. Haven't you ever discussed mother-daughter relationships with her, or with her mother when she came to see you?

What is going on between those two is not my business. Ellen making up stories about me in front of *my* mother, *that* is my business. Inventing dirt like that is a new version of her neurotic rituals. It's something you should look at next time she comes to see you. And if she bashes my mother, please remember that *I* am her real enemy, *I* am the one she's after. My mother comes in a close second though.

A stirring image it is, wouldn't you think, Ellen sitting across from her mother-in-law eating Bavarian dumplings and harassing her with invented stories about her son. It's enough to send her home right then and there. Of course, by sending her home by herself I had put myself in a quandary. How would I get to her parent's place from Toronto? She had the car, so she had to pick me up at the airport. Having to depend on her is hazardous under the best of circumstances; in this case it was tragic. Getting her to pick me up in Toronto was a serious problem for me, but for her it was a drama of gigantic proportions.

From what her mother told me I can imagine what furious battle she fought with herself when she had to decide when exactly she should leave her parent's house to get to the airport in time to pick me up. It's a six to seven hour drive from their house, so all you need to do is look at your watch, count the hours, allow an hour for heavy traffic, and that's it. My grandmother could do this, but for Ellen this was a nightmare, not because she can't tell time, but because she couldn't make up her mind if she should get to the airport early and go shopping there, or get there late to show me who is in charge. Or maybe she considered the possibility of not picking me up at all.

She left the house extra early, I was told. A couple miles outside of town she went back again, saying she had forgotten something. Then she got on the road again, only to return home again, this time to discuss with her mother the possibility of *her* driving to the airport to pick me up. Her mother refused, saying it was Ellen's responsibility to pick me up, she was old enough to drive. She had driven the car from Toronto all by herself, so she can also drive back there by herself. I should add that Ellen's mother showed considerable strength of will in this matter. Her normal routine is to cave in when her daughter makes demands. But she had changed her analyst a few weeks earlier, and her new one had told her that it was okay to stand up to Ellen. I think she should stick to this man.

The third time she took off for Toronto she turned around after she was nearly half way there. According to her mother, she was totally beside herself and refused to get in the car again. Her mother worked on her for an hour to get her back on the road. I can hear her: "It's okay Ellen, you are a big person, you can do this." I imagine she made her a cup of hot chocolate and fixed her a sandwich for the road. Doctor, I am talking about a college-educated woman who thinks she can change society by complaining to the management of hotels in Germany when she sees signs on toilet doors that show drawings of figures with skirts, rather than letters saying "Women."

I had to wait four hours at the airport for her to show up. And when she finally arrived, she was mentally worn out. This going back and forth in her mind, whether she should or should not go, be early or be late, was that an act of courage, making a decision in an emotionally difficult situation? Or was it cowardice? Was she in panic about facing me again? I don't know, and I no longer care to know.

Why do you look at me like that? No, there is no other woman ready to jump into my lap, if that's what you are thinking. That would be a bit reductive, wouldn't it? During my entire marriage there has never been another woman I was interested in. I had girlfriends *before* I met her, but from that moment on they were out of my mind. I have never asked myself how my life would have turned out if I had stayed with any of these women. And there also were no peepshows, no bars, no brothels, no gambling, nothing of that sort. When I wasn't at work, I was at home looking after my family. There were long stretches of time when I raised our children single-handedly. How much more responsible can you get, Doctor? And there has been no imagining of paths not taken, and no fantasizing about the special attention I might have gotten from the gorgeous women I met at work, at conferences, or on research travel, if I had approached them. And this is not for lack of imagination. I told you, I survive on imagination, but I never imagined being with another woman. I was too busy looking after Ellen and our kids to wander off in some other direction. If there is another woman in my head now, it is one I haven't met yet. If my children ask me, "Are you leaving Mommy for someone else?" I will say, "No," and that is the absolute truth. And what I say to *you* is that I don't need another woman to have an excuse for leaving Ellen. She is excuse enough.

No, I'm not a monster. If you want to know why giving up on her is the only solution for me, just think of your most difficult patient, someone who is just not treatable. Nothing you have tried works, none of your colleagues is helping you out, with advice or by taking over, and this patient is treating you like dirt. What would you do with a patient like this? Spend even more time with her, schedule extra office hours for her, maybe even meet her outside the office? Or would you say enough is enough, she's not treatable, she hasn't been treatable from the start? And what if she says she can't cope without you, her life is at stake, she needs you and no one else to get better, would you then send her out on the street? And if she asks you to marry her because this is her only chance to get on with life, that you owe this to her? Think of your investment in her therapy. You have gotten to know her so well, you might as well marry her, she says. Would you then marry her, *after* you officially terminate treatment of course? No, you don't have to answer this.

Some investments you have to write off before they kill you. That's what I'm doing. I'm looking after myself, I'm rebuilding my identity, my sense of self. I have been living with a person who says she'll die if I don't get her another chiropractor within the hour. How could I ignore this? And when ten doctors tell me that she needs to be able to rely on her husband, I can't brush this aside so easily. That burden is hard enough to handle, but what makes it even tougher is that *she* is the one who determines the type of support she wants me to give her. That's what she does with me. She wants me to read some magazine article about the yeast syndrome. I say, sorry, this is nuts, but then I read it anyway. She wants me to go to Mass with her, so she can pray more effectively, she says. I know this is crazy, but I go along to keep her quiet. She gets the key to my office from a secretary so she can rummage through my files while I'm out of town, and I let it go, because I have nothing to hide. She writes a letter to the mother of a girlfriend from twenty years ago to inquire about my "insensitivity towards women," and I let that go as well. Doctor, this is how it has been. I can't take this anymore, her constant nagging, do this, do that, making excuses for her, when she snaps at our children, keeping her from meddling in the personal affairs of a neighbor for doing something she finds unacceptable, and worrying whether she gets a panic attack before or after going shopping.

Do you want to know what my colleagues think when they see us at a faculty party arriving an hour late and then we leave five minutes after we get there, and half an hour later we are back again? No, I'm not making this up. This has happened more than once, and each time I came up with an explanation most people find a bit difficult to swallow: Ellen isn't sure if she turned off the oven, Ellen lost an earring on the way, Ellen needs to talk to our babysitter to give her one last instruction. Maybe I should tell them the truth for a change: Ellen isn't sure if she should take this pill before or after this party, Ellen can't decide if she should take one or two pills for anxiety, Ellen has forgotten if she has taken a pill already today.

Do you remember the panic I was in when you called me into your office to inform me that she would be getting electroconvulsive treatment. You said you were at the end of your wits, so now you would try something more powerful. That was the word you used: powerful, meaning you were applying force. Better than heavy drugs, you said, but you might as well have said that two weeks in a straightjacket is less coercive than ECT. I felt so sick from worrying that I vomited when I got home. I had the story of "One Flew Over the Cuckcoo's Nest" in my head, and I had read Sylvia Plath's "The Bell Jar." I thought of electrodes, metal plates, gagging devices, and restraining belts when you said I shouldn't worry, they would give her sedatives and muscle relaxants during the procedure, she wouldn't feel anything, and side-effects would be minimal and short-term. Still, I was horrified. I went to the library and read a good dozen research articles about this procedure to be absolutely certain that this wasn't anything like what was shown in Cuckcoo's Nest.

When I visited her in the hospital the evening before they performed ECT, I talked to her about this as if she was going to a candlelight dinner. I said that scientific studies show - with my students I never use words like show, confirm, or proof, but say that research findings suggest or indicate - that the procedure helps in the great majority of cases. And the kids are fine, I told her, they are well taken care of. I had arranged for two babysitters to be on call for the hours I couldn't be at home. So there would be nothing to worry about. I said all this to her, while I thought of our children needing a healthy mother, a mother offering emotional stability, mindful support, and loving oversight. She used to be gentle with the children. Even when she scolded them, she did it with kindness. That's all gone, her nervous breakdown put an end to it. What's left of her is a bomb. Anger, selfishness, and ruthlessness, darkness in every corner of her body.

All I can do is make sure this bomb doesn't detonate in front of our children. I am doing my best to hide what's going on, and if they do notice something, I invent excuses so they don't worry. They see their mother break out in hives, they see her hands tremble, and for everything I come up with an explanation they can understand. How often have I told them that she has a bad headache or a stubborn toothache, or that she had a scary dream? Mommy loves you, she is just not feeling well today, Mommy doesn't mean it, when she yells at you, she's just tired. I have talked to them like this for years. I lied to them, without realizing that it was myself I was telling lies to.

When I read those studies on ECT, I couldn't lie to myself. There were too many contradictions in the findings, the study populations were not described well, the researchers worked with small samples, and there were too many missing variables. And when they say memory loss is "usually" short-term, but "can be significant" and "potentially disabling in some people," and they attach numbers to these statement, like "in eighty-seven percent of cases short-term," and "in four percent of cases very significant," I concentrate on the failures, not the successes, and the unexpected findings I take very seriously. And what does it mean in practice, when a patient experiences "no change" after ECT? Would you prescribe another round of shock treatment, or move to extra strong drugs, or lock her up in an institution? Those were the thoughts I had the evening before they gave her ECT.

When I visited her in the hospital the day after she had the ECT I expected the worst. I thought I would see her sitting on the edge of her bed, her face pale and distorted from muscle spasms, holding her head over a bucket, mumbling incoherent stuff, and staring at me, as if to say, who are you, what do you want? But when she saw me come into the room, she knew exactly who I was, and there was no incoherence whatsoever in what she said to me. She was happily chatting away, while flipping through some house-and-garden magazine, smiling like someone who is thinking about a new layout for her garden next spring. And when I visited her on the second day I found her walking around the ward as if the patient lounge was her living-room. She was busy organizing leisure activities for the other patients, advising them what to eat, what videos to watch, what games to play, and what to say to their relatives when they show up for a visit. She was in charge again, she was herself. A new and improved self, or her old self, what do you think? A week later she was up and about, but the happy times lasted only a week. She was back in no time to the old routine of I-am-going-to-die-if-I-don't-do-this, and I was back in my own panic too.

Do you know how often I wished she had some *physical* problem? It's easier to live with a person who has both legs missing than to live with a hysterical yo-yo. A deformed pelvis, a broken bone, or crushed ribs are things you can see in an x-ray. You hold the x-ray picture against the light and you can say immediately where the pain comes from. But in Ellen's case the doctors said: "I don't see anything." No trace of an injury, no bruising, no lashes of the whip, nothing. Normal people would be happy to get negative results in medical tests, you say to yourself when you sit in some doctor's waiting room with her. You look at the other people sitting around you. You are angry at them. They have a leg in a cast or a bandage around the head and you think to yourself, at least they have a normal injury. And if the chest pain turns out to be nothing serious, the patient goes home with the good news: All negative! But how do you deal with someone who insists that medical tests should produce a *positive* result, or who claims that if the result is negative it's because the test wasn't done correctly? Most of our acquaintances no longer ask her about her health, because they know beforehand what she'll answer: "The doctor hasn't found it yet." Or they dress their questions in platitudes to be polite. "Trust in God," the pious ones say, while the spiritualists offer meaningless sayings like "In suffering there is knowledge." And those who can see through her say nothing at all.

I told you about the episode at that road fork in the Black Forest. Remember, I said this was a seminal moment in my life, the point when I knew that I couldn't go on like this any longer. I knew that if I continued with her I would perish sooner or later. For a second I thought about driving her to the airport right then and there, drop her off at an airline counter, *any* airline that flies to Toronto, and let *them* deal with her. Or, if there was no flight available, I'd drop her off at the Salvation Army. That sounds harsh, I know, but I was so terribly aggravated. Aggravation, does that word have any meaning for you, or would you rather hear the word despair? Because that's what I felt watching her going back and forth at that road fork until she fell apart.

Since we are talking about words, do you remember when we discussed the problem of labeling, three years ago I think it was, when you admitted her to the hospital for a week of observations. I said I didn't want her to be labeled. I know, in your profession you have to work with classifications and categories, but labeling carries its own implications. It defines the person in social space and makes him or her the object of control by others. I didn't want her to have the feeling of losing control over her life.

I have now changed my mind on this as far as Ellen is concerned. Go right ahead and classify her, I don't care anymore. She's not a cliché, you know, but nor am I. Give her some label, call her depressed or, if you want, call her hysterical, or what the wife of a colleague of mine calls her: a bitch. She's the wife of a person to whom Ellen goes for advice, or emotional support, or whatever else he may offer her. He calls her a bad girl, to his wife she's a bitch. Take a pick. These labels may not be accurate, but they give you some idea what these people think they are dealing with when they talk to her. Labeling isn't all that bad. It gives structure to a problem and thus removes ambiguity. Had you given me a label for the stuff that goes on in her head when she can't decide which direction to go at an intersection, I could have managed this situation better. Telling me that she suffers from affective disorders just isn't helpful. It's obvious that she is disturbed, but what do I do when she stops the car in the middle of the road? How does that make you feel, you say to me. Imagine I told you that you need a clear strategy for making a correct decision. Would that help you in your diagnostic decision-making?

I had intended spending a day in my mother's house as a chance for me to collect my thoughts. I didn't want my decision to send Ellen home to be an emotion-driven kneejerk reaction. Letting out that scream on the Autobahn on the first day of this trip, *that* was emotion in its purest form. If I screamed like that here in this room you would have me sedated. But sending this raging lunatic home early was a rational decision. So is my decision to leave her. I know that I cannot anticipate all possible consequences of this decision, but I don't want to end as a person who spends all day *imagining* a better future. I want to *have* that future, and that means that I need to get away from her. This is also for the sake of our children. If you are a father in a crashing airplane, you need to be the first to put the oxygen mask on your face before assisting your children.

The first thing I need to do now is check if I can return her to her parents in a form they can accept. Forgive me, this sounds like taking bad-fitting shoes back to the store and asking for a refund. Actually, yes, I *would* want to get a refund from her parents. I'm entitled to one, if you consider all that pain I went through with their daughter who, when I met her, told me that she has a "winning personality," and whose mother said to me that she is "different." They had brought her up to be "different," they set the premises for her to develop into the kind of person she is now, "winning personality" or not. So they should take her back. If you gave a patient of yours the wrong drug, wouldn't you feel obligated to offer him a refund, a couple of free sessions maybe?

If her parents don't take her back, and I have an inkling that they won't, I will move out of our house. What do you think, should I get out of this town and disappear into some distant land? It's risky, the options of continuing my career elsewhere are limited at my age. I might be able to find something in the Middle East. There are American universities with a branch campus in some of these countries, but the political situation in that region is not really what I would call academically stimulating. And why should I take the risk of getting killed by terrorists, if I have one right here at home?

Or should I give up my academic career altogether and settle in a place where she would never find me? In Kashmir, for example. There are guerrilla fighters, poisonous snakes, and nasty spiders, so she won't look for me there. It is a very picturesque area, even more stunning than the Black Forest. And it's isolated from the rest of the world, so it would be perfect for me as a hideout from Ellen. I could work as a tour guide for Americans and Europeans who are looking for an adventure of sorts. This way I might even make a significant contribution to the economy there, while also improving the understanding between nations. That alone would give me high social standing there, and this would certainly be more pleasant than the decline in social status that divorced professors in the States suffer when their abandoned wives run to the dean to denounce their run-away husband.

You know I'm being cynical, right? In Kashmir I might be safe from Ellen, but what kind of freedom would this be? Hiding high up in the mountains, freezing in bloody cold winters, struggling with thin air, running the risk of getting beheaded by terrorists, trading my relations with friends and colleagues for a chance to ride mules on stony mountain paths, and eating chapati bread all day. What a price to pay for getting rid of Ellen! I might as well stay here and live in a treehouse deep in the woods. Normal people, when they separate, go live in separate parts of the house, or they each move back to their parents, and I am talking about escaping to the Himalayas! Sure, I am being cynical. Don't worry, I won't disappear into some distant land, if for the only reason that I have two children to look after. They are too young to leave them with their mother unprotected. They need a father with a head on his shoulders. They need orderly domesticity, not a life of anger, ferocity, and despair.

After our meeting yesterday, I went to see a lawyer. It was only an informational meeting, nothing formal, just some tentative advice she gave me, and a few quite scary insights into what I will be confronted with when I separate from Ellen. She warned me that even with a formal separation agreement I shouldn't expect anything like certainty in my relations with her. The law may be clear-cut, but there are no guarantees that Ellen will act rationally, given her mental condition. These things happen all the time, she said. In situations where one or both parties are mentally unstable, judges will often let their own personal feelings enter into their decision-making, and if children are involved, things are even more complicated. If I were to leave town, even if this were for reasons having to do with my job, I should be aware that this would significantly reduce my chances of getting child custody. The children's mother would likely tell the court that I am planning to limit her access to the children. And if I would mention with one word that I might move to another country, she would argue that I would do this only to skip alimony payment. If she can get the judge to share this interpretation, I might as well forget custody. When I told her about Ellen's mental problems, she said that money will be a key issue for her. I should be on my toes and weigh my preferences very carefully. Stay in town and pay alimony, but at least see the children, or move away, still pay alimony, and never see the children again.

I asked this lawyer whether I should expect getting a better hearing in court with a formal separation agreement in place, or if I would be better off not to separate formally but simply move out of the house.

She explained that it would be easier for me to deal with Ellen blackmailing me emotionally and financially before an agreement is signed. A formal agreement would worsen my situation in this regard, as far as the law is concerned. Before an agreement is in place I can do things I won't be able to do after an agreement is signed. I could block Ellen's access to our joint bank account, for example, and I could cut up her credit card. I could also reduce my income without running into legal problems. For example, I could take unpaid leave of absence from the university, something I would like to do anyway. I desperately need a break, I am emotionally spent. Call it battle fatigue.

As the person who earns the money in this family, I can do with it what I want. She looked at me in disbelief, when I said that taking away Ellen's credit card is for me like spending family money on alcohol and gambling. Okay, she is a lawyer, so she has a matter-of-fact attitude on this, but she has no idea what I would be facing with Ellen emotionally if I were to block her access to money. Otherwise she wouldn't have said that I could get myself a girlfriend on the side, or two or three, if I felt I needed other women to feel better. From a legal standpoint this wouldn't be a problem, she said, and from a psychological perspective it might clear my head.

After I sign an agreement my freedom will be curtailed significantly in all kinds of ways. Family law is such that after separation the income earner is required to provide financial support to the weaker party. The recipient of support payments is entitled to a continuation of the standard of living she is accustomed to. And if the situation should arise that the dependent party has additional needs, the burden of proof is then on the support provider if he says he cannot pay. Given Ellen's talent for concocting fantastic stories, it should be easy for her to dream up additional requirements for her or for the children. This lawyer warned me that any action on my part after separation that would worsen Ellen's economic situation, whether intended or not, would be seen as an attempt to discard my obligations to her. Bottom line, I would be dependent on Ellen's cooperation more than ever. But cooperation is not one of her strong points, so I should avoid anything that might provoke her. I should continue being generous in supporting her, I should listen to her needs, and I should treat her with utmost respect. Sounds familiar, doesn't it?

It's clear to me that after separation, with the balance of financial responsibility shifting even further onto my shoulders, she will maintain the assumption of moral superiority all the more rigorously and all the more neurotically. Do you think I should kidnap the kids to save them from their crazy mother? I want to have control over matters of schooling and health, and everything else I need to do to care for them properly. For them it would be a clean cut from their mother. There would be some short-term pain, of course, but in time they would forget her. If I told them the truth about their mother, they would adjust all the more quickly, wouldn't you think? I could read to them some of the notes she spreads around the house in which she writes that the kids are too much of a burden for her, that she sometimes has the urge to beat them when they scream too loud.

When I brought this up with the lawyer she said that this would be insufficient evidence for me to have a strong case against Ellen in court. I would need a psychological assessment from an independent psychologist, preferably two psychologists. They would observe the children over a lengthy period of time and interview them in detail. You can expect Ellen to manipulate them so they don't speak out against her. Chrissie has already let me know that her mother depends on her psychologically. "Mommy needs me," she said to me. Ellen is sitting at Chrissie's bed, not reading bedtime stories to her, but complaining about me. And when she is in an especially negative mood, she sleeps the entire night in Chrissie's bed.

Great parenting, don't you think? Ellen, the Mount Holyoke graduate in psychology, with an A plus in her favorite subject, the creation of guilt feelings in children. An eight-year-old saying "Mommy needs me" is something that should never happen. The mother needing her child to uphold her spirits, that's a crime. A parent should teach the child life's possibilities, not vice versa. It's bad enough for Chrissie to see her mother go into the hospital once a year, but thinking that her mother needs her to feel good, puts Chrissie in an impossible situation. Her mother crawls into her bed and Chrissie says, Mommy, you can count on me. A child having to play parent will surely develop a psychological problem later in life. You don't need a degree in child psychology to know that. If interviewed by a psychologist, guess which side the child will take, because she sees me as much less vulnerable than her mother.

I have always defended Ellen in front of the kids when she played crazy. I always came up with excuses for her behavior, to explain why she is so irritable ("Mommy has one of her headaches again"), breaks out in rashes ("She got stung by a bee"), or leaves those notes all over the house ("They are just reminders of things she wants to do"). You see, I wanted my children to have the freedom to choose the kind of relationship with their mother that was meaningful to them, and seeing their mother as mentally unstable would interfere with their choice. Now I think it was a big mistake to have kept quiet about Ellen's mental problems. They cannot see how she is manipulating them, and my creativity in finding excuses for her insanity is one reason why they cannot see it. I will have to wait until they reach a certain age – thirty, forty, maybe even longer – to be able to think for themselves, independent of their mother. Or maybe they will have a partner some day who will encourage them to ask their parents a couple of intelligent questions. And then I will have things to say!

I can wait. In the meantime, all I can do is try to be coolheaded about all this nonsense, so let me tell you what I will do next. Obviously, I can't kidnap the children, and disappearing somewhere on this earth is no realistic option either. I could postpone my separation from Ellen for a while and take more freedom for myself, do things I wouldn't normally do to relax, smoke pot, for example, or get myself a girlfriend to clear my head, as this lawyer said so nicely. What will happen if I hook up with some intelligent and attractive woman, or if I take away her credit card and take a two-year leave of absence from the university without pay, and she would then quickly run out of money to make those one-hour phone calls once a week to doctors all over this country? Before I decide on this I need a good theory that tells me what she will do.

In sociology we are blessed with theories, but we still cannot explain things very well, let alone predict the future. There are always surprises and chance events getting in the way: irrational spouses, unpredictable lawyers, and biased judges. In your field you have a variety of theories too. You have Jung, Adler, and Rogers, there is classical Freudian theory, neo-Freudian, and post-Freudian thinking, and you have behaviorist and humanist approaches. Do you feel fortunate having these choices, or does it make you feel constrained? When things go wrong with a patient, do you blame theory or do you blame the patient?

How do you decide which theory to apply? Obviously, a theory must be able to explain things better than rival theories. It should be more economical and require fewer variables. It should also imply testable predictions. Ideally, those predictions should be unexpected ones, things that no one would have looked for if they were not starting from the theory to be tested. I know some of the things you have tested with Ellen, and nothing has worked. Was our outing in the Black Forest also one of your tests? I knew that the probability of this trip turning out to be a disaster was greater than zero, but I gave it a chance. So don't blame *me*.

When I asked you about the expected benefits of this outing you said I should act on faith. What kind of faith were you referring to? Ellen's religious faith? I hope not, I'm really no fan of that kind of faith. Religion isn't something for people like myself who want answers that can be tested empirically. Religion allows you to ask only so many questions before you get to the point where you have to say, well, that's just how it is, it's *because*. Doctor Birnbaum, I have a big problem with irreducible answers. What if things end in disaster? Not enough faith, bad faith, tough luck, God must have other plans, just because, or what? No, that's not how I operate. I want clarity, I want to make decisions on the basis of rational criteria.

That's why this outing was the last trip I took with her. All this going back and forth, all those hours looking for the perfect hotel, all those excuses to not embarrass her in front of other people, all this a gigantic waste of energy. My testing of hypotheses with her is over. I'm done with her. I have decided to shake that hysterical bitch out of my life. I'll look for an apartment for myself. That's what I'll do.

I don't want this to come as a complete shock to her, so before I move out I will write my own little note to her, with three copies. One goes under her pillow, one under the couch, and one in the bathroom cabinet. She should be able to find at least one of them. I have already thought about what I will write. It'll be something like this:

> "Ellen, guess what, I am leaving you. The time has come for me to look after my own needs. There will be no coming back, so don't even try going after me. And don't pull that poor-single-mother-shit on me. You won't be poor because I will pay generous alimony support to you and the children, more than what the law requires. In return I ask you, don't fuck up the children. And you won't be single if you stop harassing our friends and neighbors. I won't be around anymore to tell them you haven't slept well or that you're just having a bad day. You will either have to explain your behavior yourself or you will learn not to have bad days. I won't be there anymore to pick you up when you have a panic attack. I will be gone, so don't bother chasing after me. And *if* you do try to come after me, remember, I will always be faster than you. I will always be one step ahead of you."

Not bad for a personal declaration of independence, don't you think? Rational enough? Wait, there's more I will write:

"If you think I can't manage being my own person, independent from you, you are deadwrong. Did it ever occur to you, in the course of your ruminations, that I don't need you? I have an identity of my own, and if I haven't insisted on protecting it in the past, it's because I was looking out for you. In case you haven't noticed, I'm a *Mensch*. You understand enough German to know what that word means. It means that I'm not a slave you can order around, I'm not a houseboy you can blackmail into submission, I'm not your puppy licking your feet, and in bed I'm not your bimbo. And from now on you will have to go to your army of doctors by yourself. Your chauffeur has moved on. And don't bother 'exposing' me. People don't take you seriously when you present yourself as some biblical theater queen."

Harsh words, I know, but I don't feel any shame or guilt writing this. And here is my final message for her:

Please tell Marcus and Chrissie that I am leaving their mother, not them. That is a vital distinction, but I can't explain to them the details of it just now. They are too young for this. They would be so shattered by what I would tell them about you that they would need psychological counselling for years. What they should know, however, is that they are always welcome in my home, wherever that will be. Whatever the access rules will be, I expect you to comply with them and not to interfere in how I spend my time with the children. And as far as your own well-being is concerned, I sincerely hope that you will learn to stand on your own two feet, because there is nothing worse for one's mental well-being than having to live in economic and emotional dependence on someone else. You are the way you are, and if you want to be another person, you have to take care of that yourself. That is *your* responsibility and no one else's. In this sense, I wish you all the best."

How would that be for a goodbye note? Given her state of mind, she'll explode, but there is no way around it, she needs to hear this to know what she can expect from me in the future. Clear enough? Have I forgotten anything? I have to go now, our time is up anyway. Thank you for lending me your ear. So, goodbye, Herr Doctor. Do you want me to shut the door on the way out?

Zeitfracht Medien GmbH
Ferdinand-Jühlke-Straße 7
99095 Erfurt, Deutschland
produktsicherheit@kolibri360.de